INTO THE UNKNOWN

A TALE OF COURAGE DURING THE COLD WAR

MARION KUMMEROW

CONTENTS

CHAPTER 1

Berlin, Christmas 1948

The cold winter air swirled around Bruni's legs and she hunched her shoulders as she stepped from the crowded bar into the freezing night. Victor drew her against him for a moment to shield her from the cold gust. "You wait here. I'll get the jeep and be right back." His suggestion was accompanied by a glance at the high heels of Bruni and her friends, Marlene and Zara.

"I'll come with you," Bruni said.

"Nonsense." Victor withdrew his arm and kissed her on the lips. "There's no reason to get your shoes muddy with the snow and your feet cold. I'll be right back."

Secretly Bruni was relieved that she didn't have to brave the freshly fallen snow. She might like to watch the snow from behind a window in a warm room, but she certainly hated being subjected to the caprices of the weather.

She didn't mind standing, walking, and dancing all night in

heels so high most women wouldn't even be able to keep upright in them but she definitely could do without having to brave nature. Nature was dirty and Bruni hated getting dirty.

"It was such a wonderful concert!" Bruni's friend Zara still swooned over the Bob Hope concert, for which Glenn and Victor, both American soldiers, had gotten them tickets.

"And this bar! They had the most incredible dance music!" Marlene, the only one of the three friends who'd come solo tonight, added, "How did you know about it?"

Bruni pursed her bright-red lips and gave a husky laugh. "It's my job to know about the places with the best music in Berlin. Currently, they're springing up like mushrooms in the French sector but this one got rave recommendations from some of my regulars."

She'd deliberately suggested going someplace other than the Café de Paris, where she worked as singer and entertainer, because there they'd want her to sing. And tonight was a night to celebrate.

Not only was it Christmas day but Zara had also managed to get a flight into blockaded Berlin as Glenn's passenger, and it was the first time in nine months that the three women had seen each other.

And judging by how tenaciously the Soviet louts kept blockading the city, it might be several more months before they'd be able to repeat the reunion.

"Is that him?" Marlene asked, pointing at the headlights of a jeep coming down the street toward them.

"It is." A sudden warmth spread through Bruni's veins and took her breath away as she spied Victor's ruggedly handsome face behind the windshield. Loving someone other than herself was a new concept and it had snuck up on her in such a way she'd not even realized the extent of her feelings for Victor. Not until he'd told her he was returning to the States.

After the holidays he would ask his commanding officer for

permission to marry her, so she could follow him to America, which would be a dream come true. She'd go there to be with Victor, but at the same time she couldn't deny the allure of Broadway...or Hollywood...following in the footsteps of her famous idol Marlene Dietrich.

Victor was steering the vehicle toward them, on the other side of the street, when suddenly a half-tank that had been sitting on the curb pulled away and drove headlong toward the jeep coming down the road.

Her heart jumped into her throat and she took several steps forward, fear gripping her.

"Victor! Watch out!" Bruni yelled into the crisp night, but neither of the drivers in their closed cars could hear her. Waving her arms, she jumped up and down, intent on drawing his attention, while she watched, horrified, as the scene unfolded in front of her.

She let out a breath when Victor finally realized the threat and veered to the left to avoid hitting the oncoming vehicle. But instead of staying on its course, the half-tank aped his movement and, a few agonizing seconds later, barreled sideways into Victor.

An ear-splitting squeal pierced the air when metal scraped against metal, while the half-tank shoved the much smaller jeep forward like a plough would shovel snow until both vehicles finally came to a grinding halt on the embankment of the Nieder Neuendorfer Lake that marked the border between Berlin's French sector and the Soviet occupied zone.

"Victor!" Bruni yelled, taking another step. A hand on her arm pulled her back and all she could do was watch the surreal scene with her hand covering her slack-jawed shock. Time seemed to slow down as the half-tank backed up about half a length and then shifted gears again and crashed into Victor's jeep once more, sending it tumbling down the embankment.

Moments later, Bruni heard a high-pitched scream that

might have been hers, and the ugly splash when the jeep hit the icy waters of the lake. She stood frozen in place, unmoving even when her arm was released, aghast at the incident she'd witnessed. Glenn, though, quickly gathered his wits and sprinted down to the water where the jeep slid further away from the embankment as if it was still being driven and then ever so slowly began to sink.

Bruni couldn't tear her eyes away from the scene until she heard someone shout something she didn't understand. Her head jerked around just in time to see the half-tank reversing onto the road and racing off into the night. She followed the red taillights along the lake until it turned left and out of sight. There was nowhere to go where the vehicle was headed – except for the closed border into the Soviet occupied zone. She suddenly realized this had not been an accident at all.

Shivering with cold and anxiety, she turned her attention back to Victor's jeep where it lay half-submerged, with only the passenger cabin windows above the water line. Victor himself was nowhere to be seen, not even inside the vehicle, and her hand covered her mouth as she imagined him disappearing into the cold, murky water.

"No!" She raced forward, reaching the other side of the road just as Glenn ran into the lake.

"Glenn!" Zara screamed with horrible anguish and grabbed Bruni's left hand. Her other hand was taken by Marlene and together the three women stood breathless watching Glenn half run, half swim through the deathly cold waters until he reached the vehicle and frantically tried to open the door.

"Thank God," Marlene said, and seeing that both her friends had turned into pillars of salt, she took the initiative. "You wait here! I'll call an ambulance."

She hadn't even finished speaking when Bruni felt Marlene's hand slip from her own and she turned her head to see her sprinting back to the bar. Through the thick fog in her brain she realized her friend must be going to ask for help. Unable to do something coherent, she simply turned her head to look at the water where the jeep was slowly sinking under the surface.

Due to the darkness only lit by the reflection of the snow, she couldn't make out exactly what Glenn was doing, but with a relieved sigh she watched how he dragged Victor from the jeep and then wrapped him into his arms and carried the seemingly unconscious Victor toward the shore.

Finally her feet moved and she struggled down the embankment in her high heels and fell on her knees next to Glenn and a bruised and bloodied Victor. Some of her anguish dissolved when she saw Victor's chest moving up and down. His eyes were closed though, and blood was oozing from his forehead.

"Victor, my darling, wake up!" She was gently slapping his cheek like she'd seen people do on the silver screen, when a young man in uniform roughly shoved her aside.

Bruni was about to tell him off, when Marlene showed up beside her and touched her shoulder. "He's a medic. They've already called an ambulance and it should be here soon."

"What's wrong with him?" Bruni's famous husky voice was nothing more than a croak.

The medic ignored her, while barking orders at some American soldiers who'd been partying at the bar and had come out to help a compatriot. Someone grabbed Glenn, who was shivering violently, and said, "Come with me, we need to get you out of those wet clothes."

Bruni was too distressed to resist when Marlene led her a few steps away to sit on a small rock, and said, "We'd better not disturb the medic. He'll do his best to take care of Victor."

She nodded feebly, tears springing to her eyes. She'd never before felt such heartache as she did now, fearing she might lose Victor forever.

As always, Marlene seemed to be able to read her thoughts,

and said, "I'm sure he'll be fine. He's in the best hands and will be treated in the American Military Hospital."

Furtively blinking her tears away, Bruni gazed at her chipped nail and used this as her anchor to keep from falling apart. "Look at my hands! How am I going to fix that nail?"

Marlene had the grace not to comment, and for that Bruni was thankful, but her friend's next words made her dissolve into a puddle of appreciation at her feet.

"Look at your shoes. I'm afraid you've ruined those wonderful heels."

"Victor gave them to me just two weeks ago." Bruni sniffed and then started laughing hysterically. "Thanks for cheering me up. I'm so worried about him. What if…"

"You can't think like that—" Marlene was interrupted by the sound of approaching sirens, and seconds later two stretcher bearers emerged and carried Victor to the ambulance.

Finally, some life returned into Bruni's limbs and she jumped up, just as a jeep with two MPs arrived to get witness reports from everyone present. Bruni had no interest in answering questions, since she was set on accompanying Victor to the hospital, but one of the stretcher bearers held her back. "Sorry, miss, but only patients allowed in here."

"But…he's…my…" She fell silent. As a civilian, and German, she had no rights whatsoever to even get information about his condition, since they weren't married.

"Aren't you the singer from the Café de Paris?" he asked.

"Yes." Despite not feeling like it, she cast him the smile that made every man swoon.

He seemed to take pity on her, because he said, "Look. You can come to the American Hospital in the morning and ask for me. If I know something, I'll let you know."

"Thank you."

"My shift ends at eight; wait for me at the entrance, will you?"

"I will." Bruni inwardly groaned since she usually didn't get up before noon, especially not after a night of heavy partying into the wee hours of the morning. But to get information about Victor she'd swallow the bitter pill and forego her beauty sleep.

Bruni looked for Marlene, who was talking to one of the MPs. Glenn, in a borrowed coat, stood by her side but Zara was nowhere to be seen. Bruni walked over toward the small group, where the MP was jotting down their names and addresses.

"What happened?" the MP asked, and Glenn explained while the other man was busy scribbling down the sequence of events leading to the accident.

"It wasn't an accident," Bruni said.

"How so?" The policeman's alert eyes settled on hers.

"I thought it was, but the half-tank backed off about a half-length and then crashed straight into the jeep again."

"Were there any other witnesses?"

Glenn and Marlene shook their heads. "Sorry, no. We were several yards behind, because my girlfriend had stumbled. It all happened so fast, and when we looked up we only saw the jeep rolling down the embankment; that's when I dashed off to the waterside."

The MP turned toward Bruni. "Are you certain this is what you saw? It is a very serious allegation."

"Very certain." Despite her worry for Victor she was livid. How dare this man cast doubt on her assertion? "The driver even rolled down his window and shouted something."

"What did he shout?"

"I couldn't understand." *It sounded threatening.* She didn't say that, because even to her own ears it sounded incredible. A hysterical woman imagining things because her boyfriend had been involved in an accident.

The MP did his best to keep a straight face, but nevertheless she perceived his eyeroll, indicating he didn't believe her. "Anyone else hear what the driver shouted?"

Both Glenn and Marlene shrugged, and Glenn offered, "It wasn't in English, so I didn't understand a word."

"Well, that will be all for the moment." The MP gazed at Glenn, who looked like a drowned rat. "You sure you are okay? We can take you to the hospital."

"No, I'm fine. A ride back to the barracks will suffice, and a hot shower."

"Well then, once we're done here you can come with us." The MP turned away to ask more witnesses but, since all had only come outside after Marlene had asked them to call the ambulance, nobody had seen anything.

"Where's Zara?" Bruni asked.

"Vanished at the first sight of a military policeman," Marlene answered. Their friend had a deep-rooted fear of the authorities since she'd been abducted by the Soviet NKVD a while ago.

The MP waved at Glenn, apparently ready to return to the barracks.

"I'd better get going," Glenn said. "Tell Zara to meet me tomorrow at Tempelhof airport." Then he looked at Bruni. "I'm sure he'll be okay. I'm going to visit him first thing in the morning, and will let you know."

Bruni somehow managed to nod, even though she felt like bursting into tears. Which couldn't happen because, many years ago during her abusive childhood, she'd sworn to never again shed tears caused by a man. As soon as the policemen's jeep had vanished, Zara peeked out of the bar.

"They are gone; let's go home," Marlene said. With Bruni in the middle, interlacing arms, they steered her toward her nearby apartment in the French sector.

CHAPTER 2

Victor took a labored breath, the smell of antiseptic making his nose wrinkle and his eyelids flutter. This was so different to the smell of Bruni's seductive perfume, and it certainly wasn't her soft body pressing against him.

Instead, some heavy thing pressed down on him and poked against his lungs with every breath he took. He struggled to force his eyes open but merely saw more blackness. It must be some strange nightmare…but since when did he actually feel pain in his dreams?

He tried to stretch out to reach the light switch, but found he couldn't. He was bound in place, unable to move or even open his eyes, while people pressed down on him, embalming him alive into a mummy. Abject fear filled him and he willed his legs to move so he could run away but nothing happened.

A small corner of his brain realized this couldn't be real and he was stuck in a nightmare of the worst sort. But there was nothing he could do, except to hope that it got bad enough for him to actually wake up.

A horrible pain lanced through his leg and he let out an ear-piercing scream that finally woke him enough to open his eyes. And to close them again real fast. He was not in Bruni's bed.

"Didn't you say he was knocked out?" a male voice said.

"He was."

"He's awake now. Do you need much longer?"

"Still need to fix the other shin."

"I'll get morphine."

Victor tore his eyes open and screamed at the top of his lungs. "Get your hands off me!"

"Shush. You had a bad motor accident. The medic is giving you morphine and then I'll fix your other leg."

My leg? Was that the reason he couldn't run away? Or was this merely another layer in his nightmare and he hadn't actually woken up? Victor's head hurt too much to grasp the situation. Seconds later, he felt a prick and sometime later blissfully nothing. His face relaxed and he drifted back to semi-consciousness.

"He's ready," the younger of the two voices said.

"Well then, let's get back to work."

Seconds later, Victor felt two big hands around his lower leg and then a dull twinge. It was strong enough to make him open his eyes once more and shed some of the fog crowding his brain.

Avoiding too much movement, he let his eyes wander across the room. It took him a while to recognize the different electrical devices and cables. He was in a hospital room.

Ever so slowly, fragments of memory returned. He'd been in the jeep driving toward the bar. There was freshly fallen snow but that hadn't made the road slippery or anything. He'd had his eyes on Bruni, waiting for him, when suddenly she began waving like crazy and just seconds later that half-tank had been coming straight at him.

An image flashed through his mind but was gone before he

could grasp it. The next thing he remembered was waking up here in the hospital.

"Oh good, you're awake." The voice was the same as the one who'd said "Let's go to work," so he assumed it must belong to the doctor.

"More or less." Victor tried to move his head to see the person talking but it wasn't possible.

"Don't move; we have put your head into a neck brace, because you received a severe whiplash in the accident." The doctor moved around and into Victor's field of vision.

"How bad is it?" Victor rasped.

"Well, considering that your jeep was hit by a half-tank, and you almost drowned in the lake, I'd say you're better than we expected."

"I drowned?" Victor couldn't remember being in the water.

"Yes. You owe, big time, the fellow Glenn Davidson, since he dove in and dragged you out."

"Glenn…" A frightening thought occurred to him. What if Bruni had been injured? "Was anyone else in the accident?"

The doctor shook his head. "Just you. The driver did a 'hit and run.'"

Another image flashed through his mind, causing him to wince. "I can't remember much. I was driving and then this other vehicle came toward me. That's all."

"That's not unusual. Apart from a whiplash and slight hypothermia, you have a severe concussion, a few broken ribs, and both your lower legs were smashed by the pedals. Nothing that won't heal, given time. As far as we can see there's no internal bleeding."

Victor didn't think his condition was better than expected but it certainly could have been worse.

"Your memory will return in due course. Accident victims often shut out what happened, because it's too traumatic."

He wanted to nod but he couldn't even do that. "Can I have some water, please?"

"Sure. I'll send the nurse to look after you. Don't run away, will you?" The doctor chuckled and left the room.

Very funny. Victor couldn't even move enough to look at his feet, or anywhere else except for the ceiling and the upper third of the walls in the room.

Sometime later, the nurse brought a feeding cup and held it to his lips. "Your arms aren't broken, just bruised, so in a day or two you'll be able to hold it yourself," she said with a cheery smile as if this were a reason to be somehow happy. But then, she'd probably seen worse injuries during the war.

It seemed ironic that he'd made it through the war with little more than a few scratches, only to be caught in a near-fatal car wreck during peacetime. Swallowing liquid had been more strenuous than he'd expected and he closed his eyes again, even before the nurse removed the cup, and dozed off.

In his dreams he was with Bruni, caressing her soft skin and pressing kisses all over her gorgeous body. From the moment he'd first seen her, on stage in the Café de Paris, he'd fallen head over heels in love with her.

Her sultry voice had captivated him from the first line of the song she'd been singing: *I'm in the Mood for Love.* Even almost a year later his stomach fluttered at the memory of her wonderful blue eyes locking with his and how suddenly it had seemed she'd been singing exclusively for him.

Ever since, he hadn't been able to keep her out of his thoughts, even though initially she'd shown little interest in a relationship, because that girl didn't do love. So it was all the more wonderful when she'd fallen in love with him despite her best intentions, and after the holidays he'd planned to apply for a marriage license with his superior.

That thought caused him to wake up and stare anxiously into the night. She wouldn't be allowed to visit him in the

American military hospital, and his stomach tied into a knot wondering how long he'd have to go without looking at her exquisite face, hearing her wonderful voice, and caressing her silky skin.

He groaned in despair but thankfully the morphine they'd given him wouldn't let him wallow in self-pity for long and he dozed off again, returning to the moment the other vehicle had hit him. A man was driving…in civilian clothes…but, for the life of him, he couldn't see the face. Each time he blinked to get a clearer vision, the image blurred and faded away.

CHAPTER 3

Bruni paced across the living room for the hundredth time, only stopping when Zara reached out, grabbed her hand, and pulled her down to sit on the threadbare couch.

"Sorry."

"Don't be. I get that you're worried. I would be too," Zara said.

Bruni nodded, wrapping her arms around her chest to try and hold herself together. She was grateful for her best friend's company. Zara had accompanied her home and agreed to stay overnight, and would even go with her to the hospital in the morning to try and find out about Victor. Chances were slim but Bruni clung to the promise the stretcher bearer had given her.

"You really should go to bed; you have to fly back to Wiesbaden tomorrow," she said to Zara.

"Don't worry about me. I can sleep all I want on the plane."

"Thank you," Bruni whispered. It was unusual for her to rely on the emotional comfort of friends. Usually they came to her for advice, or even if they needed something to eat.

Early on in her youth, Bruni had vowed to herself never to

depend on anyone again, especially not emotionally. Fiercely independent and with little patience for fuzzy feelings, she'd used her two strengths, voice and looks, to get what she wanted. She had a job, miserably paid but paid nonetheless, which was more than many Berliners could say, and a string of powerful men who courted her and showered her with food, clothing, housing, and other gifts, in exchange for sleeping with them.

None of them had loved her, and neither had she indulged in superfluous sentimentality. Relationships were a business, and a very beneficial one for her – until Victor had come along. Despite her initial reluctance, because he was too low-ranking and too poor, she'd fallen for him bit by bit until she'd finally accepted that her idea of swearing off love had been flawed.

Heart, soul, and body, she belonged to him and the idea of losing him gave her physical pain.

"Here, drink this." Marlene stepped from the tiny kitchen with three cups of steaming hot tea and handed one of them to Bruni.

She took a sip and stared at the empty wall. Dean Harris, Kommandant of the American Sector in Berlin and her former lover, had arranged for her to live here, and let her stay even after he'd dumped her when his wife and children had come to live with him in Berlin. She still reeled from injured pride, since she was supposed to be the one who dumped the men, not the other way round. She took a deep breath, forcing down her rising fury. The betrayal, as she called it, hadn't prevented her from keeping the apartment, because where else would she live? Certainly not in a place with cracked walls and a shared bathroom like Marlene, or the rathole basement Zara had called home before moving to Wiesbaden in the American zone of Germany.

Her eyes wandered to the small side table in the corner with the telephone and a picture of Victor and herself during the inauguration of Tegel airport. At least something good had come out of Dean's betrayal, because otherwise she'd never have flirted with Victor…tears began violently streaming down her cheeks…as she sat there with the most anguishing heartache she'd ever experienced in her life.

"Bruni, what's wrong?" Zara's voice couldn't hide the utter shock at seeing Bruni shed a tear. At the cabaret they'd even nicknamed her the Ice Queen.

"It's nothing." Bruni wiped her tears away, struggling to regain control over her unwelcome emotions.

"I don't understand how this could happen." Marlene took a seat beside her, grabbing the cup with both hands. "Didn't he see the other car coming?"

"This other vehicle pulled off the curb and headed straight for him," Bruni said, shivering at the vivid memory.

"It was almost like the driver deliberately wanted to hit Victor's car," Zara added.

"I can't believe this. Why would anyone do that?" Marlene blew on her hot tea.

Zara, who was kneeling in front of the sofa, had a deadpan expression on her face when she began to say softly, "It was so fast but I also saw him back up and then press forward again, sending the jeep over the embankment. All of you rushed to the lake but I was frozen in place and that's when the driver stuck out his head and screamed, 'Leave us in peace, bloody American. Nobody keeps us from going on air.'"

"Leave us in peace? What a strange thing to say," Marlene mused and put an arm around Bruni. "Did Victor have enemies?"

"Not that I know about." Bruni sniffed and another tear rolled. If she didn't stop doing this she'd smear her entire makeup and look like a horrible clown. She blinked a few times, trying to come up with something, only to realize that she didn't know all that much about the man she loved.

They'd rarely talked about his work, because she found the

construction of an airport boring, and he'd hesitated to tell her about his life in the barracks, because potentially everything could be considered a military secret.

Neither had she met with any of his friends, partly because he didn't have many due to his very recent deployment to Berlin but most importantly because they'd spent every free minute alone together.

"And what does going on air even mean?" Marlene still wondered about the shouted message. "Shouldn't it be take off into the air? And didn't he do the exact opposite by being responsible for the new airport at Tegel?"

"What did you just say?" Bruni jerked her head in Marlene's direction.

"That he constructed Tegel."

"No, before that."

Marlene squinted her eyes, thinking. "Ah...that it's strange to say he's keeping them from going on air."

Hot and cold shivers ran down Bruni's spine and she slumped down looking the picture of misery. "This is all my fault."

"Don't be ridiculous. How can this be your fault?" Zara asked, her eyes wide.

"Because...he did it for me."

"Who did what for you?" Zara asked.

"Victor. He blew up the broadcasting towers at Tegel, because I asked him to." The consequences of this took her breath away. If Victor died, it was her fault. And hers alone. She had caused this whole mess.

"Bruni, you need to calm down. You don't really believe that you were the reason the radio towers were blown up. They were endangering air traffic."

"That was just the public excuse. Victor has asked me to move with him to America in the New Year. He's going to be demobilized soon and he loves me." Both Zara and Marlene looked at her as if she'd lost her mind but didn't interrupt. "I wasn't sure I believed him, so he asked me what he could do to show me he was serious. I told him to do something hard but not entirely impossible." The faintest smile crossed her face as she remembered the turbulent argument that night and their subsequent makeup sex. "He promised to silence the Russians' radio station for me. And I told him, if he could do that even for just one day, then I'd do whatever it takes to be with him. About two weeks later, the radio towers were blown to pieces. Officially at the request of the French Kommandant, but it was him. He told me."

"Oh Bruni, this isn't your fault. It's solely the fault of those despicable Soviets, wanting to oppress us. They are even worse than the Nazis were!" Zara said, getting agitated throughout her statement, which was quite unusual for the soft-spoken lithe woman with waist-length black hair who was often compared to Snow White.

Zara's father had been a high-ranking Nazi official, and thus she'd not experienced any cruelty at the hands of the former regime, but she'd paid dearly for her father's affiliations after the war and was understandably angry with the Soviets.

"But it is," Bruni said gravely. Deep in her heart she knew this hit-and-run attack was her fault and she'd never forgive herself if Victor didn't survive.

"What did this medic tell you?" Marlene asked, putting down her empty cup on the coffee table.

"Which medic?"

"The one carrying the stretcher. He stopped to talk to you."

Bruni suddenly remembered and jumped up, spilling tea over her pale green satin dress. Normally she'd have cursed, and immediately rushed to remove the stain, but tonight she didn't even care about her expensive clothing. "What time is it? I must go to the hospital."

She'd already grabbed her hat when she felt a hand on her

shoulder. "It's four in the morning; you can't go anywhere right now."

"How come it's only four?" she wondered, since it felt like many hours had passed since the accident.

"So what did the medic say?" Marlene insisted.

"He said no civilians are allowed in the American Hospital but that I could wait for him when his shift ends and he might be able to give me news about Victor."

"Glenn said he'd visit him in the morning, before we fly out. If you come to the airport with me, he can give you the news," Zara suggested.

Bruni sighed. Too many options, too many things to do. She stood, her hat in her hand, looking at her friends as if they were strangers. Zara had changed after her ordeal at the hands of the Soviets, and while she still looked like a sweet and shy young woman, she now had a hidden core of steel.

On the other hand, Marlene was a girl who always wanted to please everyone and would put the needs of others first. She was a brunette, conservatively dressed in usually the drabbest things one could imagine. Her pleasant features had adopted a perma-nent air of nostalgia after her star-crossed romance with Werner Böhm.

"You should get some sleep." Marlene got up, took the hat from Bruni's hand and led her to the bedroom, where she helped her to unzip the skintight dress and then tucked her into bed. "Zara and I are going to stay overnight. Do you have an alarm clock?"

"I guess. Look in the other nightstand." Bruni never used one, because she usually slept in, after working late nights in the cabaret. But since Victor stayed over, every time he could, he'd bought one.

Marlene found it, set the alarm and asked, "Is it okay if I sleep here, and Zara on the couch?"

"Sure. The bed is big enough." Bruni didn't care either way, she was too worried about Victor and whether he was fine.

Early next morning there was a knock on the door, just as the alarm rang. Bruni was about to hurl an insult at the idiot visiting at this ungodly hour, when she remembered, jumped out of bed and raced to open the door.

"Good morning, Bru—" Glenn's jaw fell to the floor when he perused her in nothing but her lace underwear. "Shall I wait outside?"

"Not unless I'm the first woman you've ever seen like this." She chuckled. "I'll go to my bedroom and get dressed."

He nodded, speechless, his eyes riveted to her bare skin, until she nodded at the sofa where Zara was asleep. "Your girlfriend is over there."

"I…I…am sorry," he stuttered, his face turning crimson.

Bruni loved the power she held over men, and being reminded of their attraction toward her was exactly what she needed to raise her mood after Victor's horrible accident. She sashayed into her bedroom, stepping in front of the wardrobe and pulling out the figure-hugging red dress with a less-than-decent bustline that Victor loved so much on her. It was the perfect attire to convince some poor sod to bend the rules and let her inside the hospital. And if she actually got to see Victor it would surely raise his spirits and speed up his recovery.

When she returned to the sitting room, Glenn was on the sofa, with one arm wrapped around a very drowsy-looking Zara. He cast a sideways glance at Bruni to make sure she was fully dressed, before turning his head toward her.

"Where are you going dressed like that?" he asked, looking slightly shocked.

"With you to the hospital."

"No, under no circumstances."

"Why not?"

"You'll attract too much attention."

"That is exactly what I want." She fought with herself on whether to enlighten him about how the world, and men in particular, functioned, but decided against it. "If there's any chance to visit Victor I want him to see what he's missing, so he'll do his best to heal as fast as possible."

Zara giggled. "What a warped mind you have."

"Not warped at all. It's common sense. Who's coming?" Bruni looked at Zara, who was still wrapped in a blanket.

"I'd rather stay, if you don't mind."

Marlene came in from the bedroom, wearing the same gorgeous emerald dress from the night before – a hand-me-down from Bruni. "I'll go with you if you want, although I'd rather change into something more suitable first."

Bruni gave a theatrical sigh. Her friends simply didn't understand what was best for them. With a wink at Glenn, she said, "As long as you don't need a chaperone, I won't mind it being just the two of us."

He turned crimson, and Zara asked, "What has happened between you two?"

"Nothing," Glenn hastened to assure her.

"Let's say he was a bit surprised when I opened the door."

"You didn't open it with your morning robe undone, did you?" Marlene spoke from experience. Anyone who dared knock on Bruni's door before noon would have to cope with her everlasting wrath and sometimes a much too intimate sight.

"I actually forgot to put on the morning robe." Bruni giggled, enjoying Glenn's embarrassment.

Zara shook her head. "I don't believe this."

"Hey, it's my place. I can open my door however I want."

"We really need to get going, because I have to check in at Tempelhof," Glenn said.

"Let's go, then." Bruni put on her coat, hat, and gloves and waved to her friends. "See you later! Make yourselves breakfast,

21

will you?" She walked down the stairs and into Glenn's jeep. "Thanks for taking me."

They arrived at the hospital and, as she'd been warned, she wasn't let inside; not even with flaunting her décolleté. Glenn, though, was allowed in and promised to let her know about Victor's condition.

"Tell him I love him and he needs to get well soon! And give him a kiss for me."

"I certainly won't kiss that fella!" Glenn's disgusted face made Bruni snicker.

While she was waiting, she mooched a cigarette from one of the medics coming and going, always keeping an eye out for the man who'd promised to let her know about Victor. Unfortunately, she didn't see him and couldn't even ask for him, because in her numb state during the previous night she'd forgotten to ask for his name.

About half an hour later Glenn returned, and she anxiously scrutinized his tired and worried face for cues while he signed out at the gate. Her heart squeezed tight, but when he looked in her direction he gave a thumbs-up.

"How is he?" she demanded the second he came through the gate.

"He's doing better than expected but will have to stay in the hospital for several weeks. Both his legs are broken and will probably need an operation. Furthermore, he has several cracked ribs and needs to wear a neck brace. He sends you greetings, and hopes he'll soon be able to walk and meet you outside the hospital."

"Thank you." Bruni sighed. It was good news – and bad. At least he was out of mortal danger, but it could be weeks or even months before she might be allowed to see him.

She frowned. That didn't suit her at all! She'd find a way to weasel her way into the hospital, even if she had to move heaven and earth.

"Come on, it's not that bad. He can call you from the public phone in the visitor area once he's able to leave his bed." Glenn tried to cheer her up, before looking at his wristwatch. "I should get you home, since Zara and I have to be at the airport in an hour."

Back at her apartment, they recounted the news and then Bruni and Marlene hugged Zara goodbye. "Promise you'll write?"

"I will." Zara hugged them back, and a few minutes later she and Glenn left to return to Wiesbaden.

"Honestly, I'm a little jealous," Marlene said.

"Whatever for?"

"Because she can leave, while the rest of us are trapped in this city."

"Who would want to leave Berlin, anyway? This is the capital, where all the action is." Bruni flopped onto the sofa, slipped out of her high heels and put her feet up on the coffee table.

Marlene sat on the chair opposite. "But what if the Americans can't fly in enough coal and food when winter starts and have to hand Berlin over to the Soviets?"

"That will never happen."

"How can you be so sure?"

Bruni pouted. "Because Dean said so. And as much as I dislike his ditching me for his wife, he never goes back on his word."

"He might not have a choice. Confronted with the decision to let a million people die from cold and hunger or ceding to the Russian demands, he might have to choose the lesser evil."

"Then the lesser evil would be to silently freeze in your sleep," Bruni noted sarcastically, before she closed her eyes. After a while, she said, "I need to see Victor."

"Lotte's sister works in the American hospital; maybe she could help?" Marlene offered.

"I don't think so. Glenn said I'd need a special permit, signed by the Kommandant's office." Bruni rubbed her temples.

"You're going to ask Dean?"

"Or his deputy." Bruni blew out a breath, trying not to let herself become disheartened.

CHAPTER 4

Otto Krause drove his box truck up to the checkpoint and cranked down the window despite the biting cold outside. Lately, the controls between the Soviet occupied zone and East Berlin had become more stringent and it helped to show goodwill.

A Soviet soldier approached, clad in a long coat and the typical fur cap, his machine gun propped against his shoulder. Despite crossing Allied control points on a daily basis, Otto's pulse ratcheted up a notch. One could never be too sure with the Russians. Careful not to show his nerves he put his hands flat on the steering wheel, where the soldier could see them.

"Step down," came the order and Otto slowly opened the door, always aware not to make a sudden move. Half a year into the Berlin Blockade, nerves were raw and he wouldn't be the first truck driver to be shot for an alleged threat.

He climbed down the steps, careful to keep his eyes on the soldier, and handed him the papers he kept in a manila folder, even before the order to do so came. *Never show nerves, and always cooperate,* was Otto's mantra and the reason why he rarely received lengthy examinations at the borders. That and his veiled greasing of palms if needed.

At almost thirty, he'd driven trucks most of his life, first for the Wehrmacht, then for the Americans during his time as prisoner of war and, since his release, he drove for himself. His trusted truck had been one of the abandoned vehicles lining the *Autobahn*, but with countless hours of work, bartering, and sheer determination, he'd restored it.

Drawing on the connections made in the Wehrmacht and in the prison camp he'd started his one-man enterprise of transporting anything anywhere – no questions asked. In a downtrodden Germany devoid of almost anything, his services were much in demand, earning him a modest living in addition to supporting his sickly mother.

Since he was on the road most days, his truck had become his home, although he had a room at his mother's house in the outskirts of Wittenberg. It was a convenient agreement for a bachelor: he brought her money and food, and she provided him with a permanent address, a bed to sleep in, home-cooked meals, and fresh laundry.

"Where are you headed?" the soldier asked, despite the destination being clearly stated on the transport papers.

"A warehouse in Pankow."

"Cargo?"

"Potatoes." Again, the soldier would have read this on the form that specified every detail in German, Russian, English and French.

"Let me have a look."

"Of course, officer." Otto knew what was coming, because he'd seen the glint in the soldier's eyes when hearing the word *potato*. These days, food was more precious than gold and changed hands for exorbitant prices on the black market.

He opened the box, let the soldier peruse the cargo and busied himself looking away when the man removed the small ten-pound sack positioned next to the door for exactly this purpose. The usual hundredweight would not only be too expensive, but also too heavy for a clandestine change of hands.

"Everything in order, you can proceed."

"Thanks, have a nice day." Otto returned to the driver's cab and started the motor. As always, he waited until he was well past the control post before he allowed himself to breathe out.

As soon as he arrived in Pankow, he drove onto an empty backyard and switched the number plates as well as the transport papers, putting the old ones into a watertight plastic bag and hiding them in a hollowed-out brick.

His new destination was a warehouse in Wedding, in the French sector. Due to the blockade, the Western parts of Berlin paid premium prices for foodstuffs, which was good business for Otto. Leaving the backyard, he drove toward the inner-Berlin border, whistled a song and hoped there wouldn't be any further checkpoints. Usually there were no controls inside the city, but the longer the blockade and the Allied airlift lasted, the harder the Soviets persecuted any unauthorized traffic.

Only recently they'd clamped down on foraging trips into the country carried out by desperate Berliners who bartered anything and everything with the farmers to feed their children. Just in the past week another smuggler had told him the Soviets were implementing random checks inside the capital.

While his second set of papers were in order, he feared the delay an additional control might cause – and the need for more bribes that would eat into his handsome profit.

Smuggling food to West Berlin wasn't only a way to earn money; at the same time he was defying the Soviets he hated so much. They weren't benevolent occupiers like the Americans or British – no, they were out for revenge, squashing Germany beneath their thumb. But he was also providing a service to the citizens of Berlin who'd been on minimal rations ever since the blockade had begun. Their situation would be so much worse without him and his fellow smugglers. Win-win-win all round.

He grinned, stopped whistling and raised his voice to loudly sing in his full baritone voice. As a child he'd loved singing, had even attended the choir, until the day his father had decided it was an unmanly pastime. Otto had mourned that decision, not only for the singing but also for the company of the choirboys.

Even though his father had died of tuberculosis a few years later, Otto had never returned to the choir but he loved to sing in the solitude of his driver's cabin.

As soon as he arrived at the warehouse in Wedding, his purchaser turned up, accompanied by three men who unloaded the truck at lightning speed. In their business, nobody wanted to be seen and speed was crucial.

"Hello, Franz," he said, and followed his contact into the small office, where a considerable sum of money changed hands, and they agreed on another run.

Otto received a fresh double set of papers to pass the different control points and was just about to leave when Franz said, "There's a friend needing a tour to Fulda."

"Fulda? Isn't that in the American zone?"

"Yep."

Otto did a quick calculation in his head. "That's quite a distance. It'll take me a day to get there and another one back."

"He's willing to pay well."

Despite his policy of "no questions asked", he couldn't hold back his curiosity. "What's in Fulda that you can't get from the Soviet zone?"

"None of your business. You'll be rewarded nicely, and there will be cargo both ways."

That was news. Nobody ever drove stuff *out* of Berlin, everyone only smuggled food, coal, medicine, and other daily needs *into* the city.

"So, are you interested?"

"I am. When?" As long as the pay was good, Otto was game. Times were hard and his mother's medicine was expensive, since it could only be bought on the black market.

"My friend can have your papers ready by the morning."

That was fast, even by Franz's standards. Something smelled fishy but Otto was reluctant to turn down such a lucrative business deal, while his mother's health worsened by the day.

"And the cargo?" he asked.

"Same."

"Fine. Where and when?"

Franz handed him a slip of paper with an address written on it. "Be there at seven a.m. tomorrow."

"He's going to pay me directly?"

"Yep."

Again, that was unusual, because normally all monies went over Franz's desk to make sure he got his commission.

"When?"

"You'll get half tomorrow and half when you return."

"Fine. I'll do this run tomorrow and your stuff as soon as I'm back. See you next week."

"Call me if you're delayed."

Otto shrugged. Franz and the other black marketeers liked to work with him, because he was reliable and never showed up late. He always factored in enough reserves and knew how to handle the Soviet soldiers.

Walking out of the office, he lit a cigarette and observed how the workers finished unloading his truck. Originally he'd planned to spend the night at his mother's house, a two-hour drive from Berlin, to take a much-needed bath, shave, and receive a fresh set of laundry, but since he had to be in Berlin again in the morning, he decided against it.

Instead he drove to the Schöneberg borough, where he parked his truck in an empty lot and headed out to spend a few hours in a bar. None of the patrons caught his eye and since he had to get up early and would be on the road for the better part of two days, he soon returned – alone – to sleep in his truck.

He pulled an army-issue sleeping bag and a pillow from behind the seat, took off his boots and crawled inside to get some shut-eye. The truck's windowpanes had frozen over, but the sleeping bag kept him warm enough, so he dozed off almost immediately.

CHAPTER 5

"Please, Bruni, can't you just wait until Victor is well enough to see you?" Marlene tried to talk Bruni out of her current mission.

"No. If your Werner was in hospital, wouldn't you want to visit him?"

"Certainly not. He and I broke up, remember? And since he'll never be allowed to set foot in Berlin again, there's no point to your remark." Marlene shook her head, but by the way she furrowed her brow, Bruni knew her friend was still deeply in love with the man who'd had to abandon her to save both of their lives.

"Well, Victor *is* in Berlin. And I will see him." Bruni stepped in front of the mirror to touch up her ruby-red lipstick. She was wearing an emerald green satin dress with a rose in the same material above her waist. It nicely emphasized both her thin waist and her full breasts.

"What exactly are you trying to achieve with that outfit, apart from freezing to death?" Marlene asked.

The spaghetti straps were utterly unsuitable for the winter

season, but Bruni never paid attention to such minor details. Practical clothes were for other women and she wouldn't be seen dead in sturdy shoes or a scratchy woolen sweater.

"Getting a pass to the hospital. Dean may have dumped me but he's still a warm-blooded man, as is his deputy Jason Gardner."

"You're determined to do this?"

"I am. Although…" Bruni bent down to open a drawer and fished out a pair of black silk gloves that reached up to her elbows. "Better?" She did a half-turn to look at her friend.

"I'm sure those gloves will make all the difference between freezing to death and staying nice and warm." Marlene's face showed her disapproval and once more Bruni wondered how the two of them could be best friends, when they didn't even agree on the simplest matters of clothing.

She sat down to put on nylons – a gift from Victor – and the long fur coat her first post-war benefactor, Feodor Orlovski, had given her. She wrinkled her nose. People could say what they wanted about the Russians but he'd been a good lover and had protected her from having to endure the treatment most other Berlin women, including Marlene, had been subjected to at the hands of his compatriots. Sadly, he'd disappeared without a trace after the election disaster.

She shrugged. Victor was the first man to own not only her body but also her heart. She'd fought tooth and nail not to fall for him, mostly because he had been a lowly sergeant when they'd first met – quite unsuitable to keep her in the style she was accustomed to.

"I'll see you this evening?" Bruni air kissed in Marlene's direction and left for the American headquarters where Dean and his deputy had their offices.

Since her pride wouldn't let her beg Dean for a favor, she decided visiting his deputy was the better option. Both of them kept office hours so that the German public had somewhere to go to air their grievances.

It was a nice touch, something the Soviet Kommandant General Sokolov would never do. It rankled her, that despite being the more or less official lover of one of his highest-ranking officers, she'd never exchanged a word with the General himself. *Grumpy old man!*

After presenting her identity card at the reception desk, she was let into the waiting area in the hallway. Apart from her, three dowdy housewives sat on the cheap plastic chairs. She'd rather wait standing up than dirty her fur coat with whatever might be smeared on the seats. Gardner's office was to her left but as she walked toward it, another door opened and Dean stood face to face with her.

"Bruni! What are you doing here?"

"I came to see if I could get a permit to visit someone in the American hospital," she said, preparing herself to be shot down before she even had a chance to explain.

"Is this about Victor Richards?"

Bruni nodded, and Dean gazed at her for a long minute or two. Eventually, he gestured to his office door on her right. "Come with me. I heard about his accident and I'm pleased to be able to say that, according to the doctors, he's going to make a full recovery."

Bruni followed Dean, surprised at how normal, and even supportive, he was being. "Please, have a seat."

She sat across from his desk, taking a look around. A family portrait stood on the bookshelf beside his desk and Bruni couldn't help but acknowledge how happy they all seemed.

Dean followed her gaze. "My wife and children."

"Do they like it here?"

"They do. Although, since the blockade, it's become difficult, even for us."

An awkward silence ensued. She'd rehearsed a speech for his

deputy but sitting in front of the man with whom she'd shared a bed for several months, the words vanished. Finally, she took a deep breath and said, "It might have come to your attention that Victor Richards and I want to get married."

His eyebrow shot up. "I have seen no formal request."

She had to wing it here. Victor had proposed two weeks before his accident, and they had talked about her following him to America after his demobilization.

"He wanted to wait until after the holidays. But..." she folded her hands in her lap, glad that she hadn't opened her coat to reveal her cleavage, since Dean had seen her naked too many times to fall for a bit of skin. "...this may seem unbelievable to you, given our history. I truly love Victor and can't imagine ever again spending a single day without him."

"You're right, it does seem unbelievable, coming from the woman who considers relationships merely a pleasant business transaction."

She couldn't quite tell whether he was angry, amused or simply teasing her. "I have changed."

"Indeed you have." He lit himself a cigarette and offered one to her as well, which she gratefully accepted. "The Bruni I knew would have come here dressed to kill, and not covered with a fine, but chaste, fur coat."

A heavy burden fell from her shoulders. It had been the right decision to keep the coat closed. She put a hand over her heart and added the correct amount of longing into her voice as she said, "Is there any possibility I could get a visitor's pass to see Victor? He must be in so much pain after the atrocious attack and would surely appreciate seeing me."

Dean's expression became serious. "What do you know? You are the only one who claims it wasn't an accident."

She decided to keep Zara out of the game. "That's because the others were standing farther away and couldn't see."

"You sure about this? It's a very serious accusation."

"I am." She sensed that she had to give Dean something in exchange for the visitor's permit. "When the MPs interrogated me I was too shocked and didn't remember what the other driver shouted. But since then, the memory has come back. He said: 'Leave us in peace, bloody American.'" Bruni thought it best to keep the "Nobody keeps us from going on air" part to herself, since she didn't want to divulge her involvement, albeit passive, in the whole mess.

Dean steepled his hands on the desk, but didn't answer for quite some time. She knew these minutes of silent thinking from their time together and waited patiently.

"He's not the only one to get death threats from the communists but I believe it's the first time they've actually acted on it," he finally said. "I wonder if there's more to it."

"I have been wracking my brain about this ever since the awful incident, and I believe someone was livid that he built the Tegel airport, which put a dent in the Soviets' aim to strangulate our city."

"You might have a point there. In any case, I'll appoint someone to investigate and will increase security at the American hospital." Dean studied her again for several long seconds before he visibly relaxed. "I'm glad you found love. I'll make an exception and grant you a visiting permit."

"Thank you so much!" Bruni almost threw herself around his neck, so grateful was she, but at the last moment willed herself to sit still. Prim and proper. While he'd loved her wild side when she was his mistress, he seemed to want a modest girlfriend for his subordinate.

"I'll have my secretary get the permit typed up but due to the holidays it will take a couple of days. Shall I have it delivered to your place?"

"That would be exceptionally kind." She gave him a measured smile, friendly but not overly charming, before she got up to leave his office. Just as she put her hand on the doorknob, he called out to her, "Bruni?"

"Yes?"

"I hope the two of you will be very happy together."

"I'm sure we will." This time she put on her brightest smile.

CHAPTER 6

Bruni's departure left Dean deep in thought. He liked her chutzpah and her determination to get what she wanted and, if she were a man, he wouldn't have hesitated to employ her in the administration. A knock on the door tore him from his thoughts.

"Come in!"

Jason came in and closed the door behind him, a frown on his forehead.

"What have the Soviets done this time?" Dean asked.

"Nothing. I just saw Fräulein von Sinnen come out of here. You aren't considering reviving your relationship with her?"

"Certainly not. My wife would kill me. It's one thing to stray when she's a thousand miles away but with her and the kids with me, there's no need for another woman."

"Good."

"Anything else on our agenda for the day?" Dean chuckled. Jason was his subaltern but also his best, maybe his only, friend. The position as Kommandant in Berlin was a very lonely one, especially since his nemesis Soviet General Sokolov had taken to blockading the city.

"Not really, it's rather quiet because of the holidays. By the way…the boys were over the moon about the Bob Hope concert. It was a great success for morale."

"The praise belongs to General Tunner, since it was his idea. A goodie for the troops who couldn't get leave for Christmas. Damn Soviets! If I ever meet Sokolov in a dark alley, I'm going to strangle him with my bare hands!" Dean erupted into one of his infamous temper outbursts.

Jason, though, had known him long enough not to interrupt and simply let him vent, for which he was thankful.

"If there's nothing else, I'll see you for dinner?" Jason asked.

"My wife has been hunting for the correct ingredients for weeks, so don't be late."

Jason left, and Dean attended to the visitors waiting outside his office. Today there was only a slow trickle of Germans requesting one thing or the other. When the public office hours were almost over, his secretary came in with a cup of hot coffee.

"How many more visitors?" he asked him.

"Just one man. I've already locked the front door."

"Well then, let him in, will you?" Dean leaned back to sniff at the coffee before he took a sip. The American headquarters might be the only place in Berlin where one could get real coffee and he was grateful for that. He had once tried that stuff they called Ersatzkaffee and decided he'd rather drink puddle water.

Moments later, a man in his early thirties came in, dressed in an elegant dark brown business suit and fine leather shoes. He looked vaguely familiar but Dean couldn't quite place him.

"Heinz Schuster, I'm the nephew of the owner of the Café de Paris," the visitor introduced himself.

"Please, have a seat. What brings you here to see me today?"

"Thank you for giving me a few minutes of your time. I have a business proposition for you." Schuster folded his long and slender hands in his lap. The neatly manicured fingers most certainly had never been used for manual labor.

Dean didn't let his surprise show. Usually Germans came to his office because they wanted one thing or another. Heinz Schuster was the first one to offer him something. "About what?"

"May I be frank?"

Even though he didn't like the direction this was taking, Dean nodded.

"You're a busy man so I won't waste your time beating around the bush. Certain elements are smuggling food into the Western sectors of the city. I could arrange to amplify the deliveries but would need your help."

So that was the way the wind was blowing. Dean had long suspected Heinz Schuster's uncle of doing more than a bit of black marketeering here and there. "What exactly would you need my help with?"

"If you provide me with the trucks, I can bring in enough food to feed the population through the bad weather spells when the planes are grounded. It's simply a matter of knowing how to do it." Emboldened by Dean's silence, Heinz continued, "Knowing which of the Russian guards can be in our pay and which may have to be disposed of."

Dean shook his head. "I represent the American government and as such you'll understand that I cannot actively participate in smuggling. We're going to stick it out. General Tunner has converted the airlift into an efficient operation and we can bring in all the food needed."

Heinz looked shaken for a moment but quickly recovered and said, "I'm sorry to hear this, Herr Kommandant, but may I assume that you empathize with the plight of Berlin's population and won't actively pursue those who help them?"

"Herr Schuster, I believe you know my reputation and my policies well. I have no desire to cause harm to the civilians, and there's certainly no love lost between me and General Sokolov. While I cannot support your ways, I can assure you that my priority is not to persecute those engaging in black market activities."

"Thank you for your time." Heinz stood up. "I appreciate your frankness."

Dean watched him leave and then turned to look out the window at the war-ravaged city beyond, where most buildings still showed scars from bombs and fires. No vendors stood outside on the sidewalk, wanting to sell their wares. There simply wasn't anything to sell.

If Heinz Schuster, and others like him, wanted to alleviate even a small portion of the suffering, Dean wouldn't stand in the way.

CHAPTER 7

At exactly seven a.m. Otto arrived at the given address, which turned out to be a dilapidated building with more holes in the walls than bricks. A man in an elegant dark brown suit greeted him. "Franz sent you?"

"Yes. Otto's the name." Last names were rarely exchanged in his circles, where it was best to know as little as possible.

"Good. Here are your transport papers." He gave him two sets of papers.

Otto skimmed them. "Furniture? And this is the address in Fulda?"

"Yes. They will wait for you until nine p.m. If you're delayed, call this number to make an appointment for the next morning."

"Will do." If the loaders worked quickly he'd have more than enough time to make the run and arrive well before nine to unload.

"You'll have to switch out papers and plates before crossing the border. Don't use Helmstedt."

"Why not?" Helmstedt was the nearest border town and Otto's preferred crossing because he knew most of the guards, including their standard fee. Supposedly, the Autobahn was undergoing maintenance; at least that was the official reason the Soviets had given for closing it off *temporarily,* back in June, when they'd started their blockade. Obviously, it was pure coincidence that at the very same time of the Autobahn repairs, the train tracks and waterways, connecting Berlin with the western zones, were also closed for maintenance.

What a big, fat lie. The Russian thugs wouldn't know how to repair a road if it bit them on their fat asses. He'd been on the road to Helmstedt just days prior to the closedown and hadn't seen any of the alleged damage.

About a hundred miles before Helmstedt, concrete road blocks signaled the closure of the highway and all traffic had to continue over the small and winding back streets. It was a nuisance, prolonging the travel time by at least two hours, but it was still the fastest route to the border.

He'd often toyed with the idea of running his truck through the roadblocks, just to prove the damn Soviets were lying about the maintenance work, but he wasn't crazy or suicidal enough to actually do it. There was no joking around with the Soviet soldiers.

"Because they've tightened the controls," the man said in answer to Otto's "Why not?" "Better to use the one near Eisenach, especially since your papers say the cargo is from Gotha."

Otto pictured the map of the Soviet occupied zone in his mind. It would be a ridiculous detour to go via Helmstedt up north if he was to pretend he'd come from Gotha. "Makes sense. Any advice on the border patrols?"

The other man shook his head. "Shouldn't be a problem. Trade between the two zones is still ongoing; just make sure not to mention Berlin."

"I'm not stupid, man."

"If you were, Franz wouldn't recommend you. I'm Heinz by the way, and this is just a test run. If it works to everyone's satisfaction, there will be more lucrative deals for you."

"Understood." Otto didn't trust Heinz, who was much too slick for his liking, but, then again, who *was* trustworthy in this business? "Franz said something about cargo both ways?"

"Yep. Once you've unloaded, they'll give you instructions and a set of papers for the return cargo."

"Alright. My money."

"Come into my office, will you?"

Otto hated leaving his truck alone with people he didn't know, but followed Heinz into the basement of the building, while the men started loading furniture. It was a rather odd cargo to be transporting to the American zone, but maybe it was the only kind of payment Heinz could offer in exchange for the food he was about to smuggle into the capital.

Heinz handed him a bunch of banknotes, which Otto stashed in his pocket. Later, he'd distribute them over several places within the cab as well as on his person, before he stopped at a bank to put the rest in his savings account.

"Anything else?"

"No."

Otto left the basement and walked back into the yard, where he checked that the cargo was loaded and fastened, before he drove off the holding lot and onto the street. He didn't expect any trouble at the Berlin border, since the Soviets didn't care about old furniture. As long as no vital goods reached the Western Berliners, these thugs were happy fellows. He shook his fist, exposing a tattooed snake slithering around a tree on his forearm.

Just as he'd predicted, he passed the checkpoint in Berlin without a problem and was soon on the Autobahn to Leipzig. If he hurried up he could make the detour to his mother's house in Wittenberg, wash up, change into clean clothes and eat a home-made meal. Perhaps not a meal, because his mother didn't know he was coming, but there was always bread and butter.

When he arrived, his mother wasn't home, which was even

better, since he wouldn't be delayed now by her need for long conversation. Clean, shaved, and with fresh clothes, he left her a note and money, before he served himself some food, and continued his run.

He arrived on time in Fulda, the border crossing a mere formality. Heinz had been right, down here it was so much easier than in Helmstedt. Probably, the guards couldn't fathom smuggled wares from Berlin going this far south. After unloading the furniture in Fulda, he slept in the truck and arrived the next morning at a farm where he loaded potatoes, flour, and apples for the hungry capital.

The return leg went smoothly, and he even had time to stop for a beer along the Autobahn before he reached the East Berlin checkpoint.

"Where's your bill of lading?" the soldier asked.

Otto handed over the first set of papers. The soldier scrutinized it, and gave Otto a hard glance before he waved at an approaching colleague. To Otto's relief, the new arrival was someone he'd dealt with numerous times before, much to that soldier's financial benefit.

After a brief conversation, the first soldier walked away, leaving Otto to deal with a known enemy. German marks changed hands and the man waved him on.

Otto nodded once as he put his truck in gear and drove through the checkpoint. Ten minutes later, he arrived at the hidden backyard, where he switched license plates and paperwork. Another job well done. He did some mental calculations and realized he was about to have a very profitable month.

As far as he was concerned, this blockade could go on forever. It had been the most lucrative thing that had ever happened to him, which was great, but he also sensed how the Soviets were getting increasingly desperate and tightening the controls in their efforts to shut down black marketeering.

He arrived at his destination and Franz met him, payment in hand. "Thanks. Did you have any problems?"

"Nothing I haven't dealt with before."

"Damn Soviet dogs." Franz spat on the ground. "Can I ask you to do me a favor before you leave the city?"

"I don't do favors."

"Well then, consider it a side job. You'll be paid handsomely for it, I assure you."

"It's been a rather long two days, but tell me what you need."

"I need you to make a delivery to the Café de Paris. Just Krim wine and Beluga caviar."

"Just." Otto shook his head with a huff of laughter. "Fine."

"Wait here." Franz left and returned several minutes later with two wooden crates and a nice payment in consideration of services rendered.

Otto put the crates inside the cab of his truck and pocketed the cash. In front of the posh cabaret, he parked his truck. It was already late and the place crawled with military vehicles and Allied soldiers. Since he had no intention of drawing attention to his little side business, he located the back entrance, grabbed the two crates and carried them over.

Standing in the kitchen, he asked the cook, "Waiting for a delivery?"

The woman looked up and nodded. "Wine and caviar from Franz?"

"Yes." Otto gazed at her, measuring her response and whether he could ask her for money but she seemed to read his thoughts and said, "It's already paid for. But you can go inside and have a meal and drink on the house."

"How'd you know I'm hungry as a wolf?" Otto grinned, taking off his jacket.

"Aren't you truckers always hungry?" She smiled. "Leave your jacket with me. Tell the waitress you brought the night's delivery and she'll serve you on the house."

"Thanks, ma'am." Otto hung the jacket on a hook and rolled up his sleeves to expose two arms full of tattoos. In that instant, he decided not to return to Wittenberg but stay to enjoy a night out in the posh bar he normally wouldn't be able to afford, get drunk, maybe find someone for a quick romp and then sleep in his truck.

Most of the patrons were Allied soldiers with only a few civilians among them, along with the customary crowd of pretty women vying for the soldiers' attention. He found a place at the bar and, as the cook had promised, a beer and a meal appeared in front of him.

Several minutes later, a curvy blonde appeared on stage. While he didn't care much for her looks, her voice was to die for and he wished that one day he'd be allowed to sing a duet with someone like her.

He'd almost finished his meal when a shadow fell over his plate. He looked up to recognize Heinz sliding onto the bar stool next to him.

"Otto."

"Heinz. Funny meeting you here."

"Not really. My uncle owns this establishment."

"Ah." Otto nodded.

"I'm glad I've run into you. I need another shipment of merchandise transported to the West, a week from now."

Otto calculated the time needed for his already scheduled trips and nodded. "That should work." It didn't matter what the cargo was, it was a job and Heinz had rewarded him hand-somely for the one he'd just completed.

"Good. Same address as before."

The girl on stage finished her song, and received deafening applause from the men in the audience who hooted and hollered until she agreed to an encore.

"She's an extraordinary singer," Otto said.

"And dazzling all around, but don't get your hopes up. Bruni is only interested in Allied soldiers with money and power."

"Thanks for the warning, but can't blame a guy for trying," Otto answered politely. He wasn't at all interested in the sexy woman on stage but Heinz didn't have to know that. Otto carefully cultivated the image of the tough, tattooed trucker who lusted after every big-busted girl in sight.

"Feel free to leave your truck parked in the lot outside tonight. I'll let my uncle know. Enjoy the show."

"Thanks." Otto gulped down his beer and gazed around the place. While most everyone's eyes were riveted to the singer, equally attracted by her sultry voice singing about true love and by her seductive curves, he let his eyes travel until they settled on a gorgeous hunk of a serviceman.

Young, muscled, handsome, and with the most gorgeous smile that hit Otto deep in his loins. The darkened interior of the cabaret meant he could openly assess the man and, for the first time in what seemed like forever, he allowed his baser instincts to surface, lusting over the soldier and wondering how he could possibly make his wishes come true.

CHAPTER 8

Bruni kept her special permit ready as she approached the gate at the grounds of the American hospital. The guard looked at her paperwork and directed her to a reception desk.

"May I help you?" the woman in a nurse's uniform asked.

"Yes. I'd like to see Victor Richards."

The nurse looked up with surprise. "We don't get many civilian visitors here."

"I have a special permit." Bruni handed her the paper and wondered whether she should tell the nurse that she and Victor were engaged, but decided it was none of her business.

"One moment. Let me check which room he's in." The nurse consulted a clipboard and frowned. "I'm sorry, Fräulein, that patient is not allowed to have visitors at this time."

Bruni shook her head. "Kommandant Harris personally granted me this permit to visit Mister Richards. Surely your list doesn't take that into account?"

"I will have to ask my superior. If you'd wait for a moment, please." She pointed to a waiting area a few yards away.

"Thank you, but I'd rather stand," Bruni said, after eyeing the shabby chairs.

The nurse picked up the phone. After a very brief conversation, she replaced the receiver and asked, "May I ask how you are related to the patient?"

"He's my fiancé."

"But you're not married?"

"Not yet." Bruni stifled a sigh of frustration.

"Look, I'm not allowed to give out any information…" She gazed into Bruni's desperate face, and her expression softened. "…Promise you won't tell anyone?"

"My lips are sealed."

"There were some complications and he's being prepared for a transfer to Wiesbaden."

"Wiesbaden? But how?" Even before she'd finished her question Bruni knew the answer, since the only way in and out of Berlin was via airplane. "But…he's horribly afraid of flying; he swore he'd stay in the city until the Soviets lifted the blockade."

The nurse gave her a warm smile. "There's no need to worry, he'll be sedated for the flight. There will be a doctor and an experienced nurse in the plane with him. So, rest assured that your fiancé will be in good hands and you'll be able to visit him as soon as he has recovered."

"Can't I see him now? Please? Just for a minute," Bruni begged.

"I'm very sorry, but no." A man in uniform came down the hallway and the nurse whispered in a frantic tone, "Please go. I've already said too much."

The desperation of the entire world seemed to press onto Bruni's shoulders and she all but felt crushed under the heavy weight. "Thanks anyway," she said in such a feeble voice she could barely believe it was hers.

"Is there a problem?" the uniformed man asked as he reached them.

The nurse went mute as a fish, so Bruni plastered a friendly expression on her face and said, "Not at all, sir. It seems the patient I'm looking for is not here."

She turned on her heel and left the hospital with slumped shoulders, too dejected to even acknowledge the compliments from some of the soldiers she met on her way out.

It wasn't only that Victor would be whisked off to Wiesbaden – there was a much worse threat looming over her. He'd already been approved to return stateside and they had made plans for her to follow him. And he had also planned to request an official marriage license from his C.O., as soon as the holidays were over. Getting married was the only way for her to receive the required visa to enter the United States. If he left for America, before they talked, she might never see him again.

Glancing at her watch she realized it was already late and she had to hurry up to get to the cabaret in time for rehearsals. Herr Schuster and his nephew Heinz were planning a huge New Year's party for the Allied soldiers, which included a Moulin Rouge style dance show. While Bruni herself didn't dance in the chorus, she had a solo part in the show and needed to rehearse with the rest of the girls.

Once she arrived at the Café de Paris, it seemed the upcoming premiere was the only topic the staff talked about and everyone was in an uproar over the final details, from the kitchen staff to the owner himself.

Heinz was busy procuring the fine food and drinks needed for such a spectacular event, and the irony wasn't lost on Bruni that, while the Soviet soldiers were excluded from the festivities, their country's delicacies certainly were not. Almost on a daily basis a new delivery of Krim champagne, Beluga caviar, and every imaginable variation of Vodka arrived.

"The show must go on," she said to herself as she stepped into the small changing room backstage and settled in front of the mirror, fixing her hair and putting on her stage makeup. No matter if her heart wept over Victor, she still had to go out there tonight and be the glamorous, dazzling singer everyone was clamoring for.

CHAPTER 9

Something was wrong. Victor gazed at the group of medical professionals and military personnel gathered around his bedside. Since when did a normal patient require such attention?

They'd asked him several times about the details of the accident, but much to everyone's chagrin he couldn't remember much, apart from the half-tank heading straight toward him, Bruni's shocked face as she frantically waved, the driver's head – which seemed familiar, but every time he tried to focus on the face, it faded away.

One of the military policemen said, "We're trying to assess what kind of danger you might still be in."

"Danger?" He was under the influence of painkillers and his brain felt like it was stuffed with cotton balls.

"Yes. From what we've been able to piece together, this was not just a random accident. We believe you may have been targeted by the Soviets."

"We think someone was trying to assassinate you," another man added.

"Why would someone want to kill me? I'm neither important nor famous."

"It might be connected to your role overseeing the construction of the Tegel airport."

"That's ridiculous. Tegel was finished six weeks ago. Why wait till now?"

"This is what stumps us, as well. What would the Soviets gain by assassinating you now, when the construction has finished? But we need to be careful here. We all know how tense relations have become, and we need to protect our servicemen."

Victor had no idea where this was going.

"We think you should be transferred out of Berlin as soon as possible, for your own safety. Officially, you will be flown to Wiesbaden for health reasons, because the hospital there has better facilities to treat your severe injuries."

"But...I thought... the doctor said I'm healing well."

"You are," the doctor agreed. "This is just a precaution that has nothing to do with your medical condition, but everything to do with the threat of assassination. We'll fly you out and into the American zone, where you can recover in safety. Believe me, it's for the best. And weren't you earmarked to return stateside, anyway?"

Victor nodded and Bruni's face flashed into his mind. "I need to see my fiancée and tell her where you're taking me."

"Fräulein von Sinnen was here earlier and asked to see you but we couldn't allow her to visit," the MP said.

"Why ever not?" A sharp pain shot through Victor's head. "You don't think she has anything to do with this?"

"At this stage, nothing can be ruled out."

"That's ridiculous!" Victor shot up in his bed, but sank back instantly at the agonizing pain in his chest.

"Easy. Or your broken ribs could puncture your lungs." The nurse put a hand on his shoulder and firmly held him down.

"Bruni would never! We want to get married," he said.

"That will have to wait until we have found the culprit."

"There's a plane with medical equipment leaving in forty-five minutes. The doctor will prepare you for transport and we'll escort you to the airfield." With these words, the MPs left the room, leaving only a doctor and two nurses behind.

"Can you at least get a message to Bruni?" Victor asked.

The doctor shook his head. "Our hands are tied but I'm sure you can get in touch with her once you're in Wiesbaden. Look at the positive side: thousands of Berliners would love to leave the strangling embrace of the Russian bear."

Very comforting, Victor thought.

"We'll make sure you are as comfortable as can be for the flight," the nurse said.

Only now had it dawned on him that they would shove him into one of those horrible planes that were bound to crash at any moment. Even after watching thousands of takeoffs and landings he still didn't quite trust those things. He'd sworn to stay in this cursed city until he could leave it on a train. "Can you at least knock me out before boarding?"

The nurse stared at him in disbelief. "Why would you want me to do that?"

"I hate flying." He paused, and amended his statement with, "Scrap that, I'm terrified of flying."

"What if I ask the doctor to give you a sedative before you leave the hospital? You'll still have to get on the plane, but you won't mind when it takes off." She looked at him with sympathy.

At Victor's nod of acquiescence, she said, "Don't worry, we'll get you to Wiesbaden without the slightest problem."

"Can you write a message for me?" Since both his hands were bandaged he couldn't even hold a pencil.

"If it's for your fiancée, I must refuse. For your own safety we can't give details about your whereabouts to anyone." She gave him a friendly smile, and left the room.

Victor wanted to scream with frustration. There must be a way to let Bruni know he was being transferred. He racked his brain but came up empty. Contacting her would have to wait until he was in Wiesbaden. He just hoped she wouldn't be too worried about him, or...shivers ran down his spine...or believe he'd abandoned her.

"Bruni...I love you so much...I promise we'll see each other soon," he whispered.

Several minutes later the doctor returned, poked him in a few places and asked dozens of questions.

"Doctor, I can't remember the accident," Victor finally said. "Every time I try to conjure up the driver's face, it slips away. I can see the silhouette and it seems familiar, but when I focus on the face, it's gone."

"Sounds like trauma-induced amnesia. This often happens after an accident like yours and is nothing to worry about. It won't impede your physical healing, in fact it might actually help."

"How so?"

"Keeping you from making a disturbing discovery or remembering something traumatic is the mind's way of telling the body to focus on the physical healing first."

"But...will I remember one day?" Victor asked, wanting to get to the bottom of this situation. If someone was trying to kill him, he needed to find out who and why.

"I can't say. Often with this type of amnesia, the memories return either with or without a triggering event but, on some occasions, the patient will never remember, and often doesn't want to."

"I do want to remember. So is there anything that might help?"

"Not much. Your best bet is to stay calm and relax. Stress tends to aggravate the memory loss but remaining calm and not forcing the memories to return seems to be fairly effective."

"That's counterintuitive. How can I jog my memory if I actively avoid thinking about the accident?"

The doctor smiled. "That's how our subconscious works: by disassociation. You often find the solution to a problem when doing something entirely different. That's why many people have their best ideas under the shower."

Victor sighed. He was a technical engineer and worked best with drawings and formulas, analyzing a situation from every possible angle. It was beyond him how he'd find the key to the hit-and-run accident by not thinking about it.

"I'll give you something to dull the pain, it'll also help with your fear of flying," the doctor said and whipped out a syringe. Minutes later, a welcome sleepiness engulfed Victor and he barely registered being put on a stretcher and carried to the ambulance, or the subsequent drive to the airport.

Still half asleep he looked up into the clear blue sky overhead while the stretcher bearers carried him onto the plane. His eyelids closed and he didn't fight against the sedative's effect. Instead, he conjured up the image of Bruni's lovely face and imagined her slender fingers caressing him.

CHAPTER 10

O tto parked his truck in front of his mother's small house and climbed out. He took a minute to stretch his muscles, lifted his hands over his head and rolled his neck, the popping sounds an indication of how many hours he'd been sitting behind the wheel during the past days. As he headed for the back door, the smell of roasted onions wafted into his nose.

"Mother, I'm home," he announced, as he entered the house and dropped his coat and other belongings in the hallway.

She was standing in the kitchen, her gray hair covered by a kerchief, a faded floral apron tied around her waist. He drew nearer and peeked into the pan filled with potatoes, onions, and carrots.

"Smells good," he said, kissing her cheek.

"You've been gone a long time," she said, taking the skillet off the heat.

"I went into Berlin and then did a couple of side jobs before going back to Berlin a second time. I have another job lined up in a few days from now."

"I really wish you'd take on a steady job. How will you find a girl and have a family when you're always on the road?"

"Mother...there's nothing I know besides driving a truck and killing people. What do you expect me to do?" They'd had this discussion many times, and he'd never once even hinted at the real reason why she'd never have grandchildren.

"You could work in the local mill. They are always looking for workers."

"I'd rather sit in my truck than work in that sweatshop." His mother shot him a glance and he hastened to mollify her. "My work is important, too. Someone has to transport foodstuffs from the farms to the urban centers."

"Lunch is almost ready. Go and wash up before we eat."

"Yes, Mother." But before he could walk into the adjacent bathroom, she erupted into a violent coughing fit, doubling over with pain. He helped her to one of the wooden chairs and brought her a cup of water. "Here. Drink this."

She took the cup and sipped the water, wiping away the tears formed from coughing so hard. "I'm fine."

"You don't sound fine. Did you see the doctor?"

"No." She gave him a mulish look. "There's nothing he can do, anyway. The medicine I need isn't available anywhere."

Otto reached in his pocket, pulled out a wad of bills and handed them to her. When she refused to take the money, he put it on the table and tapped it for good measure. "Go and buy the damn medicine on the black market."

"I will do no such thing. Black marketeering is a crime against the honest workers and farmers," she said haughtily.

He shook his head and sat down in the other chair. "Mother, your communist masters can't provide you with the medicine you need, but this money can. Why don't you take it, for God's sake?"

"I'd rather die an honest person than use your ill-gotten money!"

He'd never told his mother exactly how he earned his money, but she wasn't stupid and since he got paid in West mark, instead of the disliked and devalued East mark, she had obviously reached her own conclusions.

She was an easily impressed woman who believed to be a righteous Christian one must follow the letter of the law, and had thus embraced both the Nazi government and the new Soviet dictators with open arms. *Stay legal and you're a good person* was her mantra and she hadn't woken up to the fact of illegal laws or abuse of power, not even since the downfall of Hitler's Reich.

Otto himself, though, had never believed in the authorities and had gotten into trouble from early on, first with his father, then with the priest and later with most everyone else. He simply wasn't willing to obey people who deemed the likes of him an abomination of nature. A threat to mankind that had to be eradicated, oppressed or converted.

He shrugged, as he didn't like to ponder this too much, and rather rebelled against the laws. Using his fists had only gotten him into trouble, including a stint in a penal battalion during the war, so he'd started to defy the authorities in a more clandestine and profitable way.

"Look, I earned that money by providing starving people with food. How can that be a crime?"

"You're breaking the law, whatever your intentions are. A good person always obeys their government, because it's not our place to decide what is right or wrong."

"Isn't it? So, when I was a soldier and killed other men, I was a good person? But now that I help to feed starving children I'm a criminal?" He hoped to make her see the nonsense of her argument.

"Otto! Stop talking like that," she scolded him.

"Why?"

"Because the government has our best interests in mind, and even though we may not understand their reasoning at times, we are still expected to obey."

"Like we obeyed the Nazis?" If the Nazis had known about his dark secret, they'd have thrown him into one of the camps without thinking twice – what would his mother have said then? Would she still have regurgitated their smears and let her own son go to hell? Probably.

He shivered at the realization. While she had only been a half-hearted Nazi at best, she was a fervent follower of "the law", however cruel or unjust it was.

"The Nazis are gone. They deceived us all. But the communists are so much better. They have the well-being of the workers and farmers in mind. We, the common people, will thrive under the communist rule. Not like the bigwigs in the imperialist West you seem to adore so much. Why can't you be proud to be a member of a democratic association of nations under the guidance of the great Soviet Union? Can't you for once see what they have done for us?"

"Is that the smell of burned food?" He distracted her, since he knew from experience that this discussion wouldn't go anywhere. His mother was too conservative to think outside the box and she only saw what she wanted to see. But then, she'd not been to Berlin since the beginning of the blockade and she certainly hadn't been to the Western zones of Germany, so how would she know how much better off people were over there?

CHAPTER 11

B runi was ready to eat humble pie and beg on her knees if
necessary. She'd come to the conclusion that if she ever
wanted to see Victor again she had to go to Wiesbaden, but
thanks to the Soviet chokehold on her city, there was only one
way to do this: via plane.

And there were only two men in all of damned Berlin who
could give a German civilian the permission to board a military
plane. The British Kommandant, who was currently on leave in
London, and Dean Harris.

She hated to come begging for the second time in a few days,
but she'd exhausted all her other options. Their last encounter
still fresh in her mind, she put on her most modest outfit, a
black dress with standing collar and long sleeves, the perfect
attire for a funeral or to join a convent.

Next, she painted her lips in a brownish shade and carefully
smeared black powder beneath her eyes to look as desperate as
she felt. If Dean wasn't moved by her desolate face, then there
was no hope left.

When it was her turn to enter his office, she straightened her
shoulders, rehearsing once again what she was about to say.

"Bruni? What happened to you?" Dean seemed honestly shaken. She dabbed at her eyes to wipe a non-existent tear away.

"I'm fine. It's just...Victor."

"What happened to him?"

"His condition has worsened and he was transferred to Wiesbaden before I even had a chance to visit him."

His lips twitched in anger. "Oh...I'm sorry. How do you know?"

"Because the receptionist told me."

He sighed. "I assumed you'd been able to see him before the transfer."

"I need to go to Wiesbaden and be with him." She touched her curls in a gesture she had practiced countless times in front of the mirror.

"Unfortunately, that won't be possible."

"Why not? I wouldn't be the first civilian to fly on one of your planes."

"Please have a seat." He gestured toward the chair opposite his impressive desk. "I do understand your desire to see Richards, I really do, but what you're asking is impossible. Besides the bad press I'd get, when this is inevitably made public, there simply isn't a space for you."

She gazed at his handsome face and saw the slight twitch in his eyelid, which convinced her there was more to the story than he was letting on.

"What are you hiding from me?"

"Me? How did you get that idea?" Dean had never been good at lying and, with him not giving a flat-out denial of her accusation, she had proof enough that he was indeed hiding something.

"So, what is it?"

"I can't give you details, but let's just say it has to do with the Soviets."

Angry heat welled up in her. "This is about Victor and me! But no, the Russians have to butt in and make it about them! I hate them!"

It was an unusual outburst for a woman nicknamed Ice Queen, especially considering her first lover after the war had been one of the Russians she now claimed to hate.

Dean raised his eyebrows at her burst of temper. "I'm so sorry. But I'm sure everything will work out in due time."

She slumped back in her chair, seeing all her hopes dashed. "What am I to do?"

"You do what you always do. Go back to work and sing. Lieutenant Richards will recover and I'm sure he'll contact you just as soon as he is able to." Dean gave her a sympathetic look.

Bruni nodded and left his office. Instead of returning home, she walked to Marlene's place, needing a shoulder to cry on. Luckily, her friend was home and invited her in for a chat and lukewarm herb tea.

After unburdening all her sorrows, Bruni felt much better.

"Why don't you just wait like Kommandant Harris suggested? I'm sure once Victor is better he'll return to Berlin and you can be together again," Marlene suggested.

"It's not that easy." Bruni sighed, wondering whether she should tell her the plain truth.

"It seems easy to me."

"For one, he's terrified of flying."

"If he can't overcome his fear in order to see you, then he's definitely not worth it," Marlene said in a wistful tone. She was clearly thinking of her own star-crossed romance with Werner Böhm, the former SED politician turned dissident who now lived in the American zone.

"It's not just that…"

"So, what is it then?"

Bruni worried her lower lip before she came out with the truth. "Victor has already received his paperwork to return to

America. If the accident hadn't occurred we'd be applying for a marriage license by now, so that I could follow him as soon as my visa is approved."

"What?" Marlene put down her cup with a loud thump. "I thought you weren't in a hurry to get married?"

"We weren't until he got his papers. What if they whisk him away and I never get to see him again?"

"Don't be overly dramatic. He wouldn't just leave without contacting you first. It might take a bit longer but he can still arrange for your paperwork from over there."

"I need to see him. I just have to."

"Oh, Bruni...I never believed you could fall this hard for a guy." Marlene gave a small smile and cocked her head. "If the Americans won't help, what about asking the Russians? They can give you a permit to cross their zone."

The slightest sliver of hope lightened Bruni's heart as she pondered the suggestion. "I might ask Vladimir Rublev, the intelligence officer who helped Zara...but even if he gave me a permit, how would I cross their zone when all road and rail traffic between Berlin and West Germany is interrupted?"

"Hmm...good question. But I'm sure there must be ways. Maybe not going directly but via another city like Dresden or Leipzig?"

"And how would that even work?" Bruni's head was swirling with all the new information she'd received this day and she couldn't focus any longer. "I better leave. I have to show up early for work, since we're doing the dress rehearsal for the big show tomorrow. You're coming, aren't you?"

"How could I decline an invitation to the hottest show in town? Food and drinks included?" Marlene asked, and they both laughed. Every person in Berlin was much too hungry to forego an opportunity to fill her stomach.

CHAPTER 12

I t was New Year's Eve and Bruni missed Victor like she'd
miss her own leg. Tonight they'd wanted to announce their
plans for getting married...but instead she was all alone, sitting
in the changing room at the cabaret, getting ready to be the
seductress the patrons knew and loved.

Although her soul was weeping, she plastered a smile on her
face, painted her lips in a bright red and did a few vocal exercises for her upcoming performance. *The show must go on* – how
often had she or one of her colleagues said these famous words,
but today was the first time she understood what they really
meant.

Despite wanting to crawl into bed and weep, she had to go
out there on the stage, to sing, dance, and flirt. It was the night
of the much-awaited New Year's party and both her employers
and the patrons expected nothing less than a stellar performance from Brunhilde von Sinnen.

She applied an extra layer of rouge to her pale cheeks and
scrutinized her eyes for treacherous dark circles beneath them,
rubbing makeup onto her face until it looked as perfect as
always.

"It's your turn next, aren't you excited?" Ada, one of the chorus dancers, said.

Bruni faked a happy smile. "Yes, I am. I believe we've never had more people in the audience than today."

"I heard there's even talent scouts from Broadway here."

"That's great." Bruni doubted it was true, because why on earth would a scout from New York come all the way to a blockaded Berlin when singing and acting talent was a dime a dozen? Still, she decided it wouldn't hurt to put extra effort into her performance and cement her status as the undisputed star of the poshest cabaret in town.

"Your turn, Bruni! Go out and dazzle them!" the stage manager hollered into the changing room.

She closed her eyes, picturing the cheering crowd and the first line of her song, before she put on a brilliant smile and walked out onto the stage. The room lay in semi-darkness, while she and the piano player were brightly lit.

It took only a few seconds until the sad reality slipped away like a coat she'd dropped to the floor, and nothing existed but Bruni, the star, and her audience. The first line of her song, *I'm in the Mood for Love*, hit the air and the audience went quiet and listened with rapturous attention..

She remembered how she'd first met Victor and how he had complimented her on her voice as she'd sung this song, "their" song. Something shifted inside her and she imagined singing it exclusively for him, pouring her entire soul into her voice, while she pranced around the stage and flirted with the men watching her, as she'd done for years. By the time the song ended, her spirits had risen. She was the admired entertainer and her sorrows about Victor belonged in another world. A world beyond the stage.

The entire show was a smashing success and later during the night, she walked around the room, receiving compliments and praise everywhere she went. It seemed that everyone in Berlin, or at least those who could afford it, wanted to celebrate the arrival of a new and better year in the Café de Paris.

"Come join us, Bruni." Herr Schuster waved her over and handed her a glass of Champagne. She raised her glass to the group of high-ranking Allied officers, fully aware that some flirting was expected. Some time later, waitresses weaved through the room, carrying trays full of canapés with caviar, salmon, and other delicacies that weren't usually available.

Heinz arrived, and Herr Schuster took him aside so the Allied soldiers couldn't hear them. "Good job! Without that last truckload of food we would have looked like complete fools."

"Yes, thankfully there are enough Russians who value West mark more than they do ideological principles."

"Make sure we get another delivery soon, so we can stay in business."

"Sure, Uncle." Heinz raised his glass toward Bruni. "Great performance. You really do earn your salary."

She gave him a gracious nod while she tried to process what the two of them had just talked about. She'd never concerned herself before with the source of the delicacies sold to the Allied servicemen, but now it dawned on her that they must be smuggled goods.

A sudden giddy awareness spread through her veins. Where something got into Berlin there must be a way to get something – such as a person – out, too.

On tenterhooks she followed Heinz with her eyes, waiting for an opportunity to catch him alone. Much to her chagrin, though, he never was alone. He mingled with the guests, complimented the women on their looks and even danced with his girlfriend, Laura. It was infuriating and she was contemplating a ruse to get him to meet her in the dressing room when he finally headed backstage.

Bruni left the officer she'd been talking to, with a hastily uttered excuse, and hurried after Heinz, catching up to him in the kitchen, where the cook asked him to get her more supplies of caviar.

"Bruni? What are you doing back here?" he asked.

"I'd like to talk to you for a moment, alone."

He furrowed his brow but beckoned her to follow him into the dimly lit basement. "What's so important that it can't wait?"

Gathering all of her courage, she blurted out, "Can you get me out of Berlin?"

"What?" He reared back as if she'd slapped him.

"I'm sorry...I overheard you talking with your uncle and I know how you get supplies for the cabaret." She lowered her voice to a mere whisper. "If you can get things in, I thought maybe you could get someone out."

She could tell she'd completely shocked Heinz with her request. "How much did you hear?"

Bruni waved a hand and shrugged. "I don't care about your side business. I need to leave Berlin, but with the blockade that's impossible right now."

"So, wait. The blockade can't last forever."

"I don't have time to wait. I must get to the American zone and fast. Can you help me? Please?" she begged, batting her baby blue eyes and not feeling the slightest guilt over doing so.

Heinz studied her for a long time and then gave a quick nod. "I can't promise anything, but I'll put out some feelers for you."

"Thank you." She would have squealed and pressed a kiss on his cheek, but thought better of it.

"But not a word to anyone. Ever. You understand?"

"Yes."

"And now return to the party and charm the patrons into buying more champagne," he said, making a shooing motion with his hands.

CHAPTER 13

"Otto, where are you going?" his mother asked.

"Out with some friends. It's New Year's Eve," he replied, as he shrugged into his coat.

"You're going out drinking." The disapproval was visible in the twist of her lips.

"I do intend to drink a fair amount tonight, yes."

"Instead of wasting time with those friends of yours, you should be looking for a nice girl to marry. It's time you settled down and started a family."

Otto evaded answering her recurring plea and changed the topic. "What did the doctor say?"

"The same thing he says every time. He handed me the bottle of foul-tasting syrup that does nothing to stop my cough, and told me the only place to find the needed medicine is in the Western zones and with West mark."

"You still think everything is better with the communists?"

She glared at him. "Watch your mouth, Otto. Why don't the Americans sell the medicine to our doctors? I'll tell you why: Because they are inhumane extortionists."

He couldn't help but rise to the bait. "I think it has more to do with the trade restrictions between our zones."

"And why do you think they started this atrocious economic warfare? Because they are greedy bastards who hate our guts! Wouldn't you think we've had enough war and it's time to live in peace with our brother countries? "

"Actually, the Soviets started the blockade by shutting down all traffic between Berlin and the Western zones."

She gave an exasperated sigh. "I really don't know where you pick up that drivel. The Americans started this with their vile currency reform whose only reason was to destroy our economy, thinking we'd come begging to be rescued from the communists. But this will never happen. You should be grateful to the Soviets for protecting our farmers and workers, and keeping us safe from the Americans."

Otto stayed silent, since there was no reasoning with his mother on politics. She had internalized the communist propaganda spewed out by the official newspapers and radio stations. She never read a Western newspaper, claiming it was full of lies and twisted facts when, in fact, her sources of information were the ones that lied. "I'd better go. Don't wait up for me."

He headed to the local bar, waving at his former classmates as he entered, and made his way to the table they had procured. "Great that you could come, Otto." One of the men raised his beer toward him.

"I've been busy lately," Otto replied, giving his order to the waitress. He slid into a chair and greeted everyone else before asking, "What's the latest developments in town?"

Everyone started talking at once. He shook his head and held up his hands. "Sorry I asked."

Robert spoke up. "Things are going really, really well for Wittenberg. We just announced the new five-year plan for production and, I can tell you, it's ambitious. Soon enough our farmers and workers will reap the rewards and everyone will lead a better life."

"I didn't know you were an SED party member." Otto took care to keep any emotion out of his voice. Robert had been an officer in the Wehrmacht, fully behind the anti-Semite, anti-communist, anti-everyone-different Nazi mindset. Apparently, he'd shed impractical opinions as easily as a snake slithered out of its skin, and had become a devoted communist.

"It's the best thing that ever happened to me. They made me chair of the economic committee." Robert grinned from ear to ear.

"Congratulations. If you ever need help reaching quotas, you know where to find me." Despising the communist politics wasn't reason enough to deter Otto from wanting to have friends in all positions and on all sides of the issue. Those who were well connected always had a leg up in his business.

"I surely will, since we need everyone to pull together to make our zone a marvelous success. And as soon as the other zones see how well-off we are, they'll stop believing in the damaging capitalist materialism and come begging for reuni-fication."

A silence fell at the table, because nobody dared contradict the fanatical new SED official, but Otto could see in his former classmates' faces that not many believed what Robert was saying.

"Maybe the Russians could start showing their benevolence by loosening their stranglehold on Berlin," Klaus said after a while. "I'm sure that would be seen as a true act of friendship and endear the Westerners to us."

"Has anyone even seen this blockade they keep complaining about?" Stefan, another friend from Otto's younger years, asked. Stefan had been a communist way before it became fashionable and had even served time in a concentration camp under the Nazis.

Robert shook his head. "No, and nobody ever will, because it doesn't exist. The blockade is a myth, perpetuated by the Americans to show off their planes with this silly airlift. It's nothing but a scam to sell food at premium prices to starving people while preparing for the next war, this time against the peaceful Soviet Union and her brother countries."

"I don't know. Do you really think the Americans would go to all this trouble and cost just to show off?" Klaus commented.

"Well, Otto, what about you? What do you think about all of this?" Stefan asked, putting him on the spot. "You've been driving your truck through our zone and into Berlin on a weekly basis."

"Have you seen this blockade?" Klaus wanted to know.

To prevent himself blurting out how much nonsense the SED had spewed, Otto gulped down his beer. "I don't know, I see lots of things. What exactly does a blockade look like?" he finally asked, making a joke of the conversation.

A few snickers here and there indicated he'd succeeded with his plan but, just in case, he called out to the waitress, "Another round on me!"

"You have money burning a hole in your pocket?" Klaus asked, with a smirk.

"It's New Year's and I'm here to get drunk!" Otto wouldn't tell his comrades that every West mark he earned equaled four to eight East marks when exchanged on the black market. There wasn't much to buy in the Soviet occupied zone, but at least it was dirt cheap when you earned your money in hard currency.

Given a choice, he'd let the blockade stick around until he had a nice nest egg saved up. Then he couldn't care less if the Americans and the British decided to start World War Three with the Russians. He'd be well set up and out of the fray by then.

CHAPTER 14

"Where's Bruni?"

Bruni lifted her head upon hearing her name and looked toward the dressing room door. "I'm right here."

"Can you come to my office for a minute?" Heinz asked, before ducking back out.

"In a moment." She finished painting her lips with the bright red lipstick and went to join him in the small windowless room he and his uncle used as an office. It was crammed with furniture, crates, paperwork and whatnot, but she didn't let her eyes wander, because for the last five days she'd been sitting on pins and needles to find out whether he could help her.

He cut right to the chase. "Still want to get out of Berlin?"

"Yes. The sooner the better."

"For how long?"

She hadn't actually thought about this and looked at him, puzzled.

"I mean, when will you be back at work?"

"Oh..." Bruni took a wild guess. "I think I'll need a few days at most, plus travel time. I'd be back within a week."

He rubbed his chin. "My uncle won't like this at all."

"I think I can make it in five days…and I haven't had a day off in months."

"Okay, ask him about leave, but don't mention my name or that you're planning to leave Berlin."

"Understood." Bruni got the message bright and clear. Herr Schuster wasn't privy to this and might even sabotage it, should he get wind of it.

"There might be a way for you to leave the city and return, but it's going to cost you."

She nodded and then swallowed hard at the number he stated. "I don't have that much money saved."

"You can pay in kind."

"What exactly are you thinking about?" It shouldn't surprise her that Heinz would ask for sexual favors, although she'd never seen him with any woman other than his girlfriend Laura. He got up and locked the door before he came toward her.

"Here and now?" she asked.

Heinz laughed. "I'm not interested in perishables."

If she weren't so desperate for his help she'd slap him. Boss or no boss, nobody insulted Brunhilde von Sinnen.

"I rather thought about something more durable. Like that beautiful necklace of yours."

Her hand flew to her neck, where a golden necklace with a small diamond lay. Feodor Orlovski had given it to her. While she had no emotional attachment to the necklace, she certainly knew how much it was worth on the black market. "That is extortion."

"It's only extortion when I force you to do something, but, if I remember correctly, you came to me begging for my help." He returned to sit behind his desk, scrutinizing her. "What will it be?"

She sighed and removed the jewelry from her neck, dropping it into Heinz's outstretched hand. He took it between his fingers and scrutinized it from all sides before he said, "It's even more precious on closer inspection. It must have once belonged to a truly rich and classy woman."

Her lip twitched for a split second and she swore to one day take revenge on him for this remark. For now, though, she smiled sweetly, pretending she hadn't understood his barb. Should he believe she was nothing but a stupid cabaret singer, since it often came in handy to be underestimated.

He pocketed the necklace and pushed a heap of papers over the desk for her to take, while he explained, "You live in Wittenberg and have been visiting your ailing aunt in Berlin. These papers give you a free pass everywhere in the Soviet occupied zone."

"And across the border?" she asked.

"You'll have to wing it. Border controls down south aren't strict. The so-called *Kleine Grenzverkehr*, locals crossing the border on a daily basis, isn't heavily controlled and the trucker who will be taking you is known to the police. Pretend to be his girlfriend and you'll be fine."

"He'll drive me all the way to Wiesbaden?"

"Nope. Just across the border to Fulda."

"And then?"

"Then you're on your own."

She glared at him. "I would think paying with a diamond necklace should give me the entire trip."

"You thought wrong. Prices have skyrocketed since the Soviets' last slew of measures to halt smuggling." He looked at her in a completely detached way, as if they were talking about bus fares and not her paying him an outrageous price for his help to cross the Soviet occupied zone.

"Fine." She gritted her teeth and pocketed the permits. What choice did she have? It wasn't as if many people lined up to offer transport into the American zone. "When and where do I meet the trucker?"

"The day after tomorrow at seven a.m. right here on the parking lot."

Seven in the morning? Heinz must be positively insane. He knew she worked late into the night and most days didn't go home before three or four in the morning.

"Well then, I'd better get ready for my performance." She walked to the door and shot back the bolt just as he reminded her, "Don't mention my name in this."

"I won't." She gave him a measured smile. "Your uncle wouldn't be too pleased, I assume." *Nor the authorities.* Then she left the room with her head held high.

The next day she packed a small suitcase, taking plenty of time to choose her wardrobe since she wanted to look her best for Victor. Excitement filled her body as she thought of his reaction when she showed up at his bedside, intent on making him forget all his pain and sorrow.

She packed several pairs of high heels to go with the dresses, and her jewelry, just in case. Depending on how things worked out she might not return to Berlin for a while. In the afternoon she visited Marlene and told her about the great news.

"But what are you going to do once you reach Wiesbaden? How will you get into the hospital?"

"I don't know yet, but I'll find a way," Bruni assured her. "Maybe Zara can help?"

"I wouldn't count on that. She wasn't even able to help herself when Glenn was in the hospital," Marlene reminded her.

"Well, I'm not going to let such a minor detail stop me. One problem at a time. First, I need to cross the stupid Soviet zone and get to Wiesbaden. The rest I'll deal with as it comes."

"Shouldn't you let Victor know you're coming?" Marlene asked.

"It's not like I can call him, right? And a letter will be much too slow, I'll be there before the mail even leaves Berlin."

"That's right." Marlene gazed at her friend. "And he'll just love the surprise."

"Thank you." Bruni felt the tension leaving her. Secretly, she'd been worried whether it was the right thing to do. Victor wasn't the spontaneous type and liked to have everything planned in advance.

"When are you leaving?"

"Tomorrow morning."

"That early?" Marlene frowned. "I'm going to miss you."

"It's not like I'll be gone forever," Bruni assured her, although she wasn't certain how or even when she might return to Berlin. Or if she wanted to.

"Have you at least called Zara to alert her to your arrival?"

"I tried, both from the cabaret and from home, but the phone line wouldn't connect." Phone service between Berlin and the western zones was sketchy at best. The copper cables were constantly overloaded and preference was given to military calls.

"I thought the new beam antenna the post office installed a few days ago would mitigate these problems..." Marlene ran a hand through her hair.

"It must be too cold for it to work."

"I don't think this technology is susceptible to temperatures."

"What do I know? Fact is, the phone didn't connect."

"Victor would know," Marlene said, since Victor was an engineer in the American army.

"See? One more reason to go and find him. I'll be sure to let you know about his evaluation of the phone line situation." Bruni giggled and was serving herself another glass of the red wine she'd brought, when the door opened and Marlene's roommate Lotte arrived. "What are you celebrating?"

"Nothing." Bruni shrugged.

"Then what is the wine for?" Lotte hadn't known Bruni long

enough to be accustomed to her always having things others couldn't afford.

"Actually, I think we should celebrate." Marlene beckoned for Lotte to sit on the couch. "Take a glass."

"What do we toast to?" Lotte asked.

Bruni exchanged a look with Marlene, reminding her that the journey to West Germany was top secret, and then she shrugged. "The fact that we made it through an awful year and are still alive?"

Lotte burst into giggles. "Really? Fine. Let's celebrate those two things; God knows I haven't got anything to celebrate."

"Still no word from your fiancé?" Bruni asked. Lotte was desperate for news about her boyfriend Johann, who was a Russian prisoner of war.

Lotte shook her head. "No. They are releasing more and more prisoners each day. I keep hoping that one day he'll show up on my doorstep."

"It will happen." Marlene took her hand, and Bruni raised her glass. "Let's drink to Johann's swift return."

Thinking about it, Bruni was in a much better position than Lotte, who didn't even know for sure whether Johann was still alive, let alone where he was and when he'd return.

After emptying her glass, Marlene got up and returned a moment later with a letter in her hand. "Will you do me a favor and give this to Werner? He works at the American radio station in Wiesbaden."

"Sure." Bruni got up and embraced her friend. "I have to go, don't want to be late for work." She still had to talk to Herr Schuster and ask him for leave, although she intended to take this trip no matter what he said.

"Take care." Marlene held her tight, while Lotte cast them a suspicious glance and murmured, "You two are up to something; I can smell it."

CHAPTER 15

Victor watched the nurse stretch his leg up, the pull on the muscles more pain than pleasure. "Ouch!" he called out when she stretched it too high.

"That's enough for today." She put his leg down. "The doctor should be in to see you in a few minutes. I'll be back tomorrow."

"Great," he told her with no enthusiasm. He hated being in the hospital. Upon arrival in Wiesbaden he'd undergone several operations to fix the smashed bones in his legs, which had shattered all his hopes of leaving this place in a matter of days.

It was driving him crazy to lie around doing nothing. The nurse had even refused to arrange for a colleague to bring him a drawing pad so he could work on some engineering problems, because the doctor had ordered complete bed rest and, supposedly, engaging his mind on work problems would somehow hinder the healing of his legs. Thank God he wasn't a medic, since believing in such superstition wasn't something his technical mind could do.

The door opened and the doctor walked in, taking his mind off his stationary existence for a few minutes. "We had to insert a screw, called a *Küntscher-Nagel*, into your lower left leg to stabilize the bone."

"A metal screw?" Victor asked in disbelief. This must be one of the most ridiculous things he'd ever heard, and he was sure the doctor was kidding him.

"Yes. It's one of the few good things to come out of Germany. In 1939, a doctor called Gerhard Küntscher fixed a complicated femoral fracture with a metal screw and, as it was such a success, it was widely adopted after the war."

"I'm now some kind of robot with metal parts?" Victor tried to make light of his condition.

"Only temporarily. We'll have to remove the bone screw several months from now."

"Oh." Victor didn't relish the idea of another lengthy hospital stay with even more operations, but it seemed nobody cared about or even asked for his opinion.

"There are two MPs outside who insist on speaking with you. Are you up for that?" the doctor asked.

"Sure." It was a welcome distraction in his boring routine.

"Very well. I'll ask them to be brief." The doctor opened the door and two MPs walked in and approached Victor's hospital bed.

"Second Lieutenant Richards. We have a few more questions," one of them said.

"Go ahead."

"Have you recalled the face of the driver who struck you?"

Victor shook his head. "No. Every time I try, the same thing happens. I can see the vehicle and the driver, but where the face should be there's nothing but a grayish fog."

Victor looked at the doctor, who had stuck around to supervise his patient. "I dream about it every night. I climb into the jeep and then I see these bright lights coming straight at me. I hear the screech of metal on metal and feel my jeep rolling down the bank into the lake. I can see through the windshield into the other vehicle, I can even see that the driver was wearing a dark-colored shirt."

"Does he seem familiar?"

"I don't know. Sometimes I think I know him, but when I try to get a clear view, he disappears," Victor told them, frustration in his voice. "Why can't I remember?"

"It'll come in time. The nightmares and cold sweats will go away with time, as well," the doctor assured him.

"If you remember anything, send word to the command center and we'll interrogate you again," the MP said.

"I will. I'd like to see the culprit pay for what he did to me."

"About that. We have reason to believe it was a deliberate attack from the Soviets, which is why you were flown out of Berlin."

"What?"

"It wasn't safe for you there. And, while you're much better protected outside the Soviet zone, we still want to keep your whereabouts a secret and therefore you can't talk to anyone without security clearance."

It took a few moments for Victor to understand that he was not only grounded, but also forbidden to receive visitors. "What about my fiancée? Can I at least get word to her?"

"Is she that singer in Berlin?"

"Yes."

"I'm sorry, but no. We aren't one hundred percent sure she isn't involved."

"That's ridiculous! Bruni would never!" He wanted to sit up in bed but pain in his ribs made him sink back against the pillow.

The doctor scolded the MPs. "I said no excitement. The patient needs complete rest."

"Sorry," the MP said to the doctor before he turned to Victor again. "Our hands are tied, since she's a German civilian and in Berlin."

"Can you at least let her know I'm alive?" Victor asked with a deep sigh of resignation.

"I'm sure she already knows, because she somehow managed to get a pass for the hospital in Berlin. Luckily, she arrived too late, when you were already being transferred to the airport."

Victor didn't share his opinion that it was lucky. He must have looked very miserable, because the second MP, who hadn't said anything so far, took pity on him. "You can contact her as soon as we have caught the culprit."

"Can I at least get a visit from a colleague?" he asked.

"Who is it?"

"Glenn Davidson, captain in the air force and airlift pilot. He's stationed in Wiesbaden and was with me before the accident. Maybe seeing him might jog my memory?"

The MP glanced at the doctor, who nodded and said, "From a medical point of view this might actually be helpful."

"Well then. We'll give Captain Davidson permission to visit you."

With these words they were gone and Victor was alone again. Miserable because of his injuries, but even more so because he couldn't get word out to Bruni.

It wasn't until the next day that the door opened and Glenn strode in. "You look like you're in a funk."

Victor snorted. "You'd be too if you were grounded and not allowed to have visitors."

"I'm a visitor, am I not? They even rescheduled a flight so I could come here." Glenn grinned. "How are the nurses?"

Under normal circumstances Victor would have thrown the pillow at Glenn, but since every movement hurt he decided to let it go. "They won't tell Bruni where I am."

"I heard."

"So did they tell you this ridiculous suspicion that someone tried to assassinate me?"

Glenn's eyes narrowed and his usually jolly face turned serious. "It's not at all silly. Zara told me the half-tank drove right at your jeep, and afterward the driver yelled 'Leave us in peace, bloody American. Nobody keeps us from going on air.'"

Victor felt the blood draining from his head. "Holy shit! If that's true..."

"Why would she make it up?"

"Did she tell the MPs?"

Glenn shook his head. "She's too afraid of any kind of police after what happened to her, but Marlene reported it the day after it happened."

"That's why they were so eager to get me out of Berlin."

"And of Germany. Apparently, you'll be flown out to the States as soon as you can leave the bed."

Ripples of frustration rushed through Victor's veins. He absolutely had to see Bruni before that happened.

"Man, you must help me. I need to get word to Bruni or I might never see her again."

"Why don't you write a letter to her?"

"They don't want anyone to know where I am."

"If you tell her that you're okay, without mentioning a location, I'll take the letter to Berlin and see that she gets it."

"Man, you're a true friend. How can I ever thank you?"

Glenn grinned. "Is it true you had those darned radio towers blasted because of her?"

"Partly. I mean, she gave me the idea, but it wasn't hard at all to convince the French commander to give the order. He'd probably have done it anyway, just a few weeks later."

"You're really in knee-deep."

"I love this woman with all my heart." Victor felt a happy lightness warming his aching bones.

Glenn fished pen and paper out of his breast pocket and handed it to Victor. "Here, let her know you're okay, but make it quick."

"Thanks, man."

My love Bruni,

Please rest assured I'm well and can't wait until I hold you in my arms again. Whatever happens, I will contact you and we will get married.

Love always,

Victor

He read the letter once, folded it in half, and then in half again.

"Finished?" Glenn asked.

Victor nodded. "Thanks for doing this."

"No thanks necessary. Get some rest. I'll visit again as soon as my schedule allows."

When Glenn left the room, Victor turned his eyes to the window and wondered what Bruni was doing. Since she was a night owl, she might not even be up. A smile crossed his face as he imagined her slender body half covered by the bedsheets.

CHAPTER 16

Proud that she was only five minutes late, Bruni arrived at the cabaret's parking lot completely out of breath. It was empty, save for a large box truck at the far end, which had to be her ride across the Soviet occupied zone.

She'd taken great care with her outfit, wanting to impress Victor when she finally saw him tonight. Inwardly, she cursed Heinz for his awful idea of meeting her driver here, while fighting to hitch up her tight, knee-length, cream-colored, sequined dress beneath her coat, so she could step across a puddle without dirtying her five-inch heels.

Nobody else was here, which was no surprise, given the ungodly hour. The cabaret didn't open its doors to the public until early evening and even the kitchen employees, who were always the first ones to come to work, wouldn't show up before noon.

Focused on evading the puddles as she traversed the graveled lot, she started when a deep voice said, "Smack my ass and call me Sally, if you aren't the singer."

She gazed up at the man standing a few feet away from her. He was a rough character, tall, broad shoulders, hair much too long, and a beard. Despite the cold, he was wearing nothing but a shirt with the top buttons open. Thick chest hair peeked out and a tattoo crawled from under the neckline of his shirt and up the side of his neck.

"You wouldn't know where I can find Otto?" she asked.

"I'm Otto."

"Very funny. I'm supposed to meet him here." She made to bypass him and walk to the back entrance but he stepped into her way, his eyes sparkling with amusement.

"If you're Bruni, then you've found your man."

Realization trickled in and she barely smothered her gasp of dismay. When Heinz had said trucker, she hadn't expected to see...this. Although, if she was being honest, all the truckers she'd ever met looked exactly like this. So, why had she expected anything else? She forced a pleasant expression on her face and offered him her hand. "Very pleased to meet you. I'm your passenger."

He looked her up and down before his gaze fell on her high heels. "Where do you think you're going with those?"

"That's none of your business." God, what an insufferable brute he was. Victor had better show undying appreciation for all the sacrifices she was making to see him.

"It's very much my business, since you're riding with me. Those shoes may be suitable on stage but not in my truck."

"That is your problem, not mine." Bruni couldn't stand this sort of guy. He apparently believed the world belonged to him and everyone, including her, had to do his bidding.

"It's very much my problem if the Soviets stop us, because you're dressed like a tart and they'll want to feel you up." He smirked.

"I don't know why it would concern you but if you wish to approve my outfit, here it is." She opened her fur coat and, out of pure malice, did a twirl on her heels so he should get the full picture and salivate over her figure.

"You're not riding with me dressed like that."

"Excuse me?" Bruni declared haughtily.

"You heard me. I'm not taking you dressed like that," Otto said. "So, if you still want the trip, I'd suggest you change. And make it quick."

"I am not changing...Otto, wasn't it? What I am wearing is perfectly acceptable attire."

"For the cabaret, maybe. Not for traveling unnoticed across the Soviet zone."

She looked down at the dress she'd chosen that morning with the glittery sequins sewn in swirling patterns across the bodice and skirt. She liked it because it brought out the platinum color of her hair and made her eyes shimmer in an azure blue. The caramel fur coat she wore on top was not only gorgeous but had the added benefit of keeping her warm.

Adopting a mulish expression, she crossed her arms over her chest and said, "I paid well, so you're going to take me, whether you approve of my outfit or not. Besides, if you don't like this dress, I doubt you'd like anything else I brought either." She held up her suitcase to emphasize her words. "My closet was fresh out of dungarees and wellingtons."

Without giving him a further glance, she stomped to the passenger side of the truck and struggled to climb up into the cab, until she felt a hand on her backside shoving her upwards. When she regained stability, she turned to give him a scathing remark, but Otto had already disappeared.

Moments later, he jumped behind the wheel, chuckling, "Told you, you should have changed into something more practical."

"I don't do practical."

"Too bad. But do me a favor and stay inside the cab at all times, will you?"

"I certainly don't have any intention of mingling with any trucker friends of yours."

He gave her a sideways glance as if he were about to say something, but didn't. Bruni relaxed a bit and leaned back in her seat. If this Otto didn't expect her to make conversation, she might as well catch up on her missed beauty sleep.

"Wake up." He prodded her shoulder, blowing cigarette smoke into her face. "We're about to reach the Soviet zone checkpoint. Better button up your coat and put on a friendly face."

"I know how to deal with soldiers," she retorted, annoyed about his patronizing ways. Did he think she was born a popular cabaret singer? That man had no idea! Instead of judging her for rising above the poverty and misery of her youth, he should take a hard look at his own life and why he'd stayed in the gutter and become a trucker.

He blew a cloud of smoke into the air while steering the heavy vehicle with his left hand. The craving for a cigarette overwhelmed her and she waited a few minutes for him to offer her one, since her own were packed in the suitcase, which was now out of reach behind her seat.

But of course the uncouth brute didn't know the first thing about good manners, so she finally asked, "Would you have a cigarette for me, too?"

"Extras are not included in the fare."

She was about to issue a scathing remark, when she noticed the twinkle in his eyes. Under different circumstances she might have appreciated his humor, but after getting off on the wrong foot with him, it only infuriated her more. Even when he handed her a lit cigarette she was not mollified.

CHAPTER 17

It was the first time Otto had taken a passenger with him. Normally, he worked alone, since most of his runs weren't strictly legal. Having a person on board made it all the more likely to slip up and get caught. And the Soviet police tended to charge by the person, which meant every control point got more expensive.

Although, when Heinz had mentioned the very generous payment, he'd made an exception. But holy shit! This woman was a spoiled princess if ever he'd met one and he wasn't sure they would finish the trip without him murdering her and dumping her body somewhere along the way.

From the moment he'd spotted her dressed like she was getting on stage, he'd known she meant trouble with a big T. Yeah, he'd immediately recognized her as the lead singer from the cabaret, but refused to let her know how much he admired her extraordinary voice, since she was arrogant enough already.

Though, he quite enjoyed her witty retorts and the way she refused to take crap from him. In other circumstances, he could imagine becoming best friends with her. But he was too proud to break the icy silence in the cab, and waited for her to make the first move. An apology would be nice, too, although he didn't count on her doing the decent thing.

Deep in thought, he gazed at the dashboard, gave a start and blinked several times, but nothing changed. The needle on the temperature gauge was climbing like mad and about to hit the maximum.

He cursed, blinked again, just as the needle hit the end stop.

"What's wrong?" Bruni asked.

"Don't know, temperature going up like crazy."

"Really? I'm still cold," she said and wrapped her coat closer around her.

Otto merely rolled his eyes, since he had neither the time nor the inclination to explain to Miss Haughty that he was talking about the engine temperature. She'd probably ask him what an engine was. He pressed on the brake and pulled off to the side of the road.

"Stay in the truck. I'll go and check," he said, grabbing his jacket and jumping down into the slush edging the road. He opened the hood and tucked his head beneath to assess the problem.

"What's wrong?" Bruni asked from his left shoulder.

"I thought I told you to stay in the truck?"

"And I thought I could help. What is the problem?" she asked, stepping like a stork across the patches of ice.

Otto peered up and down the road, checking for traffic. The last thing he needed was other cars stopping and watching the show Bruni gave in her high heels and glittery dress.

"Look, lady, we really don't want to draw attention to us. Get back in the cab."

"I do need to stretch my legs. It isn't exactly comfortable in there."

He grouched, "Sorry that I couldn't provide a limousine. Will you at least close the coat over your dress, please?"

Bruni smiled when he used the word "please" and he

smirked over the fact he'd found a way for her to do his bidding. Even the haughtiest woman had a soft spot. She buttoned up the coat and asked, "Happy now?"

"Yes." He wasn't, but this was probably the best he could expect, and the faster they got onto the road again the less chance she had to attract the wrong kind of attention.

He put his head back beneath the hood and soon identified a torn fan belt as the culprit. "Great!" Without the belt the engine would overheat and might even get damaged, and of course he didn't have a spare one with him. If he let the engine cool down and then crawled at low speed to the next repair shop...

"Did you find the problem?" Bruni asked.

"Hey, lady." He looked up to give her a piece of his mind but her fine legs caught his attention. "Are you wearing stockings?"

"What kind of question is that? Any decent woman does."

"What a lucky man I am to have a decent woman as my passenger. Would you be so kind as to give me one of your stockings?"

"Certainly not." She glared daggers at him and he couldn't help but laugh at her antics.

"No worries. I'm not interested in you but the fan belt has torn and I need a replacement to get us to the next garage."

She gave him a puzzled look. "So why don't you go ahead and put the spare part wherever it belongs?"

"Thing is, lady, I don't have one. But one of your stockings would make a fantastic fan belt."

Her eyes became wide as saucers when the realization hit her. "Do you even know how much these cost?"

"Sorry, I don't. Would you rather sit here and wait a few hours for the next police car to come by?"

"No need," she hurriedly said, and he felt a twinge of satisfaction at her obvious discomfort, although it was beyond him to understand how someone could be so attached to the thin and transparent hosiery that wouldn't even keep her warm. She glanced around, leaving him at a loss to know exactly what the problem was.

"Where can I change? Or do you expect me to undress out here in the open?"

A long chuckle escaped his throat. "I didn't think you'd mind. But if you'd rather not, then use the back of the truck." He walked around the vehicle, opened the back door for her and helped her up.

Some time later, she handed him one stocking through a crack. It was a fine, shimmery stocking and he whistled through his teeth. His engine pulleys had never seen a finer fan belt.

Once he was sure they could continue their journey to the next workshop, he wiped his hands on a rag and climbed behind the wheel. Bruni was sitting in the passenger seat with a funny look on her face, shivering.

"Once we get driving, the heating will go on again," he said, feeling sorry for her.

She didn't answer until they were several minutes into their journey. "Do you know what's in the back of your truck?"

Otto shrugged. "Old furniture."

"Did you know that between the pieces of old furniture are valuable paintings and antiques?"

"And your point?"

"I'm one hundred percent sure this is contraband. Probably stolen by the Nazis from whatever museum and now whisked away to some rich investor overseas."

"Lady, I hate to disappoint you, but who exactly do you think would smuggle a person out of Berlin?" He gave her a sideways glance and relished the shocked expression on her face. "No, don't answer. If you haven't noticed, I'm a blockade runner. Normally I transport food from the Soviet zone into West Berlin. It's my way of defying the Russians and helping to feed people. But once in a while I transport other stuff. That's my job. Drive things from point A to B. No questions asked."

She looked at him, the worry clearly evident on her face. "What happens when the Soviets catch you?"

"Nothing. The border patrols get their palms greased to turn a blind eye and let me pass. It's as much to their benefit as to mine, because those rank-and-file soldiers don't earn much."

She seemed to be satisfied with his answer, because she relaxed back into her seat and closed her eyes. There was no reason to be worried. He'd done this stuff ever since the capitulation almost four years ago, and knew his way around. The blockade had been a godsend, giving him more business than he could handle.

"This is different though," she suddenly said, several minutes later.

"What's different?"

"The stuff you're transporting."

He snapped at her, "Can't you just sit back and shut up?"

"The Americans may turn a blind eye to food smuggling, but they sure get their hackles up when it's about stolen art. And not to mention the Russians with their fixation on anything they consider cultural property, which of course is their way to say they want to sequester the items away to Moscow."

"Nobody will notice anything."

"It took me less than a minute." Her triumphant smile rankled him.

"That's because you were sitting on that sofa to take off your stocking." He had to risk a glance to find out whether she'd taken off the second one, too, but couldn't see anything because she was wrapping the coat tightly around herself.

"Every idiot would see this. If you're lucky and the border patrols are as dumb as you paint them, you might get away... although if they're only half as greedy they'll see their chance to make a lot of money."

He pondered her words, not liking the implications. He knew as well as everyone what would happen if the authorities found out. And the prospect of disappearing behind bars forever was very troubling.

"Damn it." He slammed his hand down on the steering wheel. "I knew something was off. We shouldn't even attempt to cross into the American zone."

"Oh no! Please, don't do that," Bruni begged him.

"You know if they catch me they'll arrest you as well, right?" he asked. "Who the hell is after you, that you're willing to risk that?"

"Nobody is after me." She gave him an indignant look. "I just need to visit someone in Wiesbaden."

"Your dying mother?" He thought of his own mother. He and they might not be on the best terms and she might not understand him, but he'd still do anything for her.

"No." Bruni gave a weird frown. "My parents are long dead to me."

He sensed there was more of a story to that, but resisted acting on his hunch to know more. Something told him Bruni would bare her claws if he pressed for information. "So, what's the hurry?"

"He's a soldier and if they send him back to America before I get there, I may not see him ever again." She made such a forlorn-dreamy face, his resolve to dislike her melted. He hadn't pegged her as the type of girl who would lose her heart over a guy. He was himself a complete sucker for romance and love stories. Probably because he'd never get his own happy ending due to his type of love being forbidden.

"You sure seem to love this man."

"Very much so." She chuckled self-deprecatingly. "I know that's hard to believe coming from someone like me...believe me, I was just as shocked as you look right now when I realized what I'd allowed to happen. But there's no cure for true love."

"Look, lady, the fan belt needs to be fixed properly. We'll have to stop at a garage before we can continue our journey."

"But we're still going?" she asked.

"For now." He withdrew his pack of cigarettes and extended them toward her. "Want one?"

"Thank you." She took one and held it while he lit the end and they silently smoked, each lost in their own thoughts.

CHAPTER 18

Bruni sat in silence as Otto drove. Despite the first impression, he wasn't such a bad guy. Obviously way beneath the kind of man she usually mingled with, but with a heart of gold hidden under that tough exterior.

She wondered whether he had a steady girlfriend or one in every town like a sailor had in every harbor. Wasn't that what men did? Even those like Dean, who dearly loved their wives, needed a mistress to keep them warm during prolonged times of separation.

About an hour later, they drove into a small town and he parked in front of a gas station that doubled as a repair shop and a bar.

"I'll talk to the mechanic, you go on inside and have something to eat. The food is good and cheap."

"You come here often?"

"I try to avoid roadside breakdowns." He grinned. "But I probably know every waterhole along all the major roads in the Soviet zone."

She cocked her head. "Don't you live in Berlin?"

"No, lady. Berlin is for the fancy ones like you." He threw his cigarette stub to the ground and stepped on it to extinguish the glow, before he headed toward the garage, leaving Bruni to her own devices.

She wasn't hungry, but could certainly do with a coffee, although judging by the shabby appearance of the building she might have to settle for a beer. It was almost noon and the parking lot was full of trucks.

At least she wouldn't be alone in that sad excuse for a restaurant, and while truckers were known to be a salacious bunch, so were soldiers. And Bruni's specialty was handling raucous men. As soon as she stepped inside, warm, smoke-filled air, with the distinct smell of goulash soup and beer, made her feel right at home.

Before working at the posh Café de Paris, she'd earned her keep by singing in every shady bar that would pay her, most times with nothing but a meal to fill her empty stomach. Those days were long gone; nevertheless she felt a tug of nostalgia. Not that she wanted to return to that life, but more as a reminder of how far she'd since come – from the street urchin who'd run away from her abusive father, to the much admired star singer at the most-praised cabaret in Berlin.

She hung her coat on the rack by the door and headed straight for the long bar, fully aware of heads turning to stare as she passed the patrons and hoisted herself up onto a bar stool.

"A coffee, please."

"Sorry, love, just ran out of coffee," the big-busted, tired-looking waitress said.

"Well then, I'll have a beer and a schnapps." It was always a good idea to order hard liquor to wash away any awful taste or smell. It took little more than a minute before the first man sauntered over to hit on her. Bored after the long and mostly silent drive with Otto as her only company, she decided to indulge him.

Emboldened by her reaction, more men gathered around

her, intent on impressing the strange woman with the glittery dress. Bruni was in her element, immensely enjoying the attention.

"So what does a pretty little gal like you do for a living?" one of them asked.

Bruni batted her lashes and leaned forward, whispering, "I sing."

"Hear that, fellas? We have a songbird amongst us."

"Sing something for us, sweetie."

"Yeah, now the ball is in your court! Sing for us!"

"Sing. Sing. Sing. Sing," the men chanted, and before she could object, two of them hoisted her up, bar stool included, and carried her over to the corner, where they sat her down on a small stage. A shabby place like this didn't have a piano, or even a microphone, but Brunhilde von Sinnen didn't need one.

Her trained voice could easily fill a room and silence a group of rowdy men. Slipping into her role as entertainer, she grabbed an imaginary microphone and began to sing. It didn't take more than a few notes before the entire audience were enthralled with every sound that came from her lips. It was a nice distraction from the otherwise boring trip through the dull and dreary Soviet zone.

She stepped off the bar stool, walked around the stage and flirted with her audience. Completely thrilled by the admiration of the men, she forgot where she was and launched into her usual evening program at the cabaret, cheered on by boisterous applause from her captive audience.

After some time, Otto burst through the doors and stormed toward the stage, yelling, "What do you think you're doing?"

"I'm singing, or what does it look like?" He had no right to behave like a jealous lover.

"I can see that, you crazy woman." He grabbed her wrist and dragged her behind him toward the door. It was so humiliating that he behaved as if she somehow belonged to him, and he had the right to have a say in what she did or did not do.

"Otto! Let me go!" Bruni tried to wriggle her wrist from his hand, but the grip was too tight. "You big oaf! Stop it!"

The men behind her, who'd been flirting and praising her talent before, now cheered Otto on, advising him to keep a tight leash on his woman so she didn't wander off again.

Bruni boiled with rage. How dare this brute treat her like an impertinent child? Even worse, why did her audience switch loyalty in the blink of an eye and take his side? It just showed that men weren't to be trusted, except maybe Victor, who was the big exception and had never let her down.

"Please, Otto, let me go," she pleaded, her voice sweet as honey, but he ignored her, which in itself puzzled her. Men normally fell at her feet – but he seemed to be completely immune to her charms.

Without letting her wrist go, he grabbed her coat with his other hand and pushed her through the door. Only when they had reached the truck did he ease his grip.

Just to show him how very uncouth his behavior was, she rubbed her wrist, moaning in pain. "Look what you did!"

"I'm sorry, I didn't mean to hurt you." At least he had the decency to look contrite. But just as she launched into a tirade about his unacceptable behavior, he put his big, smelly hand over her mouth and said, "Shut up, will you?"

When she nodded her agreement, he removed his hand and shook his head. "Are you trying to get us arrested? What in the world were you thinking? We're supposed to keep a low profile and you go into that bar and put on a show? Don't you think every man in there will remember you if asked by the police?"

"I was bored," she said, crossing her arms over her chest in defiance, although a twinge of guilt made her bite her lower lip. It probably hadn't been the wisest thing to do. Not when she was here under false pretenses and with a truckload of smuggled goods.

"Yeah, well, considering what we just discovered, you need to be content with being bored. It might keep us both alive a while longer," he groused.

"I guess we'd better leave now?" she said, utterly ashamed of her behavior. She'd never wanted to put them in danger.

"We can't. They don't have the proper fan belt and have to get it from the next town, which they can't do during peak hours."

Bruni pursed her lips. "So, what's the problem? We take your truck and drive there."

He shook his head. "No. I don't want to risk another roadside breakdown. It's better to stay here. They allowed me to park the truck behind the garage, where passing police won't see it."

She gave him a suspicious gaze. "How long, exactly, will they need to fix that whatsit thing?"

"It's called a fan belt."

"Thank you, but I have no desire to become an auto mechanic."

"And here's me thinking it could be a future profession for you."

She had to laugh. "Okay, you win. So, how long will we have to stay in this miserable place in the middle of nowhere?"

"I wouldn't count on leaving before tomorrow morning."

"What? I counted on being in Wiesbaden by tonight," she yelped.

"Sorry if that doesn't fit with your travel schedule. Even if we are terribly lucky it won't be fixed before nightfall. And I'd rather not drive at night. Too many bored police on the roads."

"We have to stay here overnight?" Bruni could already imagine that she'd have to sleep in the passenger seat, sharing the threadbare blanket she'd seen in the cab with Otto. What a horrid outlook.

"We do."

She didn't dignify him with an answer and stormed off toward the pay phone on the side of the building, but before she could put the coins into the slot, Otto was beside her hanging the receiver back on the hook.

Seething with fury, she wanted to give him a piece of her mind, but he preempted her. "Just making sure you're not doing something stupid."

"And what could that possibly be?"

"Giving away our location."

"Oh." Her shoulders slumped a little. "I'm not really used to this illegal stuff. I just wanted to let my friend know that I'm fine."

He studied her for a long while, and then said, "Go ahead. Tell her, but don't say anything else. Nothing about the cargo, or the breakdown, or our location."

She nodded, giving him a hint of a smile. "I wouldn't even know the name of this forlorn place."

"Even better. I'll be over there if you need me." He pointed toward the garage and left.

Bruni placed a call to Marlene, who'd recently gotten a telephone line to her place, but the operator let her know that due to maintenance there was currently no service into West Berlin.

Fuming, she hung up and placed a call to Zara's employers in Wiesbaden. Again the operator informed her that due to maintenance…She slammed the receiver onto the cradle before the woman had finished her sentence. It seemed the Russians hadn't just cut off all traffic of people and goods, but also the exchanging of words.

She grumbled in frustration as she walked toward the garage to find Otto. He was standing next to a man smeared with oil from head to toe, chatting animatedly.

"Did you speak to your friend?" Otto asked.

"There are no lines into Berlin."

The oil-smeared man gave her a brooding gaze. "Strange, that. My wife called her aunt in Lichtenberg last night."

"But that's in…" *East Berlin.* She didn't finish her sentence, because Otto cast her a warning glare. *Damn Soviets!* "…I guess I'll try again later."

"You put on quite a show, I'm told," the burly man said, and hastily rubbed his hand on his dungarees before offering it to her. "I'm Ludwig Hertz but everyone calls me Lutz. This place is mine."

"My pleasure, Lutz," Bruni said, shaking his hand while doing her best to hide her disgust with the oil dirt and smell.

"I'd better get back to work. You'll find my wife, Maria, behind the bar if you need anything." He wiped his hands on his dirty dungarees once more and walked into the garage.

"Lutz has offered to let you sleep in the storage room above the bar, since there's no guesthouse nearby. Go grab your suitcase from the truck and his wife will show you the room."

It was still early but Bruni had no intention of repeating her experience with the bar patrons and decided she might as well lie down and catch up on her lost beauty sleep. Together, they walked behind the building where his truck was parked out of sight and he took her suitcase from the cab.

"What about you?" she asked him.

"I'll sleep in the truck."

"Are you sure?"

"Wouldn't be the first time this week," he said, and when he noticed her surprised face, he added, "I have everything I need to turn that thing into a semi-comfortable bedroom. It's what we truckers do when we're on the road."

"Well then, I'd better go." She took the suitcase from him and walked away. But after a few steps she turned around, and said, "Thanks. It seems I misjudged you. You're not such a bad guy."

He laughed heartily. "Is this supposed to be a compliment, my oh-so-gracious lady?"

Hiding her own amusement, she quipped, "It's as good as you'll ever get from me. Goodnight."

She walked into the bar that was now eerily empty, since the dinner time rush hadn't yet begun. Maria was already waiting for her behind the bar.

"Hey, love, Lutz said you gonna sleep here."

"Yes, that is so very kind of you."

"Would you be interested in giving another show tonight? We'd split the extra profits with you."

It was a tempting offer, but she politely declined, because it didn't bear thinking of how Otto would react. "I'm sorry, but I'm very tired. Maybe another time?"

"You can always come here if you need a job. The men were enraptured by your voice. And enraptured patrons spend more money." Maria might look like a girl from the boondocks, but she sure had the shrewd sense of a successful business woman.

Maria beckoned Bruni to follow her up the stairs into a dilapidated room that truly deserved the label of storage room, because it was filled to the brim with junk and trash, including a metal bed in a corner with a moldy-smelling mattress on top.

"Sorry I can't offer you anything better," Maria said, but Bruni waved it off. Even though it had been many years ago, she'd slept in worse places.

"Thank you. It'll do. It's only for one night."

"If you come downstairs in about two hours, you can have a meal and I'll give you a fresh towel from the kitchen."

Bruni nodded her agreement despite being unsure whether it was wise to take Maria up on the offer and appear downstairs. Maybe when the crowd was gone and nobody would see her.

CHAPTER 19

Otto watched Bruni disappear into the bar and looked back at his disabled truck. It wasn't just the unexpected delay that bothered him, but the hot load of stolen art. Transporting needed goods into blockaded Berlin was one thing, but this could actually send him to prison for a long, long time.

He opened the back to see for himself. At first glance it was just wooden furniture as the transport papers said, but now that he knew, he distinguished not only the antique chairs and tables, but also the chandeliers, tapestries and paintings that were certainly worth a lot more than the paperwork claimed.

A cold shiver ran down his spine. He was no newcomer to the prison experience and certainly didn't want to repeat it, especially not in one of the infamous high-security prisons where the Soviets incarcerated and tortured the so-called enemies of the people: traitors, dissidents, and the like.

Surely someone who smuggled precious cultural heritage, as the Soviets called it, wouldn't be treated with kid gloves and might even be whisked away to a Siberian gulag. Rumors abounded and none of them were good. He'd seen the German prisoners of war returning from the Russian camps after years in captivity and every single time he'd thanked God that he'd been captured by the Americans.

His time in the POW camp had been no bed of roses either, but compared to what those lads had endured...he shrugged off these troubling thoughts. The truck was safely parked out of sight and as soon as the new fan belt was installed, he'd leave for Fulda and get rid of the hot load. But one thing was sure, he'd never in his life work for Heinz again.

He jumped down and locked up the back of the truck, before he headed into the bar for a meal and a drink, hoping Bruni wasn't pulling another newsworthy spectacle in his absence. The truckers were a tight bunch with no love lost for the police but he couldn't bear to even contemplate what would happen if the villagers got wind of the attractive singer and flocked to the place.

"Hey, Maria, what's for dinner tonight?" he asked.

"Goulash soup or potato stew."

"I'll have the goulash and a beer." He walked through the crowded place, greeting a few acquaintances, before he recognized two fellow blockade runners.

"What's up?" he greeted them.

"Wanna sit with us?"

"Sure, why not?" At least with them there would be no talk about the virtues of the communists or ridiculous claims that no blockade existed and it was all an American publicity stunt.

He secretly eyed one of them, a burly, muscled lad a few years younger than Otto, but he knew better than to show an interest, as he didn't know for sure about the other man's sexual inclinations. Better to give a wide berth to everything that even remotely smelled of trouble, right now more than ever.

Maria showed up with his order and set it down in front of him. "Your pretty singer never showed up again."

"She must be exhausted from the journey."

"You take your girlfriend with you?" one of the men asked.

"This is an exception." Otto thought it wiser to let them believe Bruni belonged to him. "How's business?"

"Doing well. That blockade was a godsend except for those poor devils, the Berliners. Have you heard the English are flying out children who are severely undernourished?"

"Are they?" Otto hadn't known they transported civilians and wondered why Bruni hadn't taken the easy way and flown out.

"Yes. It seems there's a long line of children waiting to be taken to relatives in the West to feed them up."

"I really don't know how long the Americans will hold up the airlift. It must cost them an arm and a leg."

"Sure does, but they'd do anything to keep the Soviets from taking over. Once this rotten pack has all of Berlin they'll take the rest of Germany and Europe as well."

"And then it'll be 'good night, nurse'."

Otto nodded. None of the blockade runners was a fan of the Russians and their oppressive methods for shoving communism down everyone's throats. "Let's hope the Soviets will fold and be forced to stop their blockade."

"But not just yet, I need the money for a down payment on a house."

The conversation soon turned to powerful engines, bothersome police patrols and, inevitably, to the topic of women. Otto ordered another beer, listening quietly since he had nothing to contribute on that subject.

"I need to get going," he finally said, knocked on the table and left the bar for another night in his truck.

The next morning, he was up before the sun climbed over the horizon and maneuvered the truck into the oversized garage, where Lutz was waiting for him with the new fan belt.

"Nice one," Lutz commented, removing the stocking and throwing it at Otto, who caught it with one hand.

"I doubt the lady will ever use it again." The stocking had

suffered badly and he disposed of it in the garbage can. Then he paid Lutz for his services, including the meals, and said, "Good work. I'll go and wake the lady, we need to be on our way. Should have delivered the load last night."

"Tough business, always in a hurry. Maria is overjoyed to have me home every night."

"Aren't they all?"

"She's a real looker, that girl of yours."

"She certainly is." Itching to get on his way, Otto left to wake Bruni.

CHAPTER 20

A sharp rap of knuckles on the loft door jolted Bruni awake.

"There's water on this side of the door so that you can wash," Otto called. "Get a move on. I'm ready to get out of here."

Bruni sat up and looked out the tiny window. The sun was nowhere to be seen but the sky showed a faint blue stripe on the horizon. It seemed to have become a – very unwelcome – habit to get up before noon.

If she weren't in such a hurry to reach Victor she'd give this brute a piece of her mind. Still grousing, she slid from the bed and headed for the door in her transparent negligée. She hesitated for a split-second but then thought, *To hell with Otto, he shall get an eyeful.*

But when she opened, there was nobody to be seen. From downstairs she heard the clatter of pots and pans, which reminded her of last night's missed dinner. She picked up the pitcher and brought it inside, noting that whoever had filled the pitcher had included a small cloth and had even heated the water.

She made short work of freshening up, redid her makeup

with the tiny mirror she kept in her makeup case, and carefully combed her hair. It absolutely needed a thorough wash, but a good brush and hair clasps had to suffice. Who could have known that a simple trip to Fulda would have meant spending the night in some dilapidated truckers' waterhole?

When she was satisfied with her hairdo, she turned her attention to the open suitcase and the very limited wardrobe she had to choose from. She pondered her choices, knowing that no matter what she wore, Otto would throw a fit. A mischievous smile crossed her lips. If he was to find fault with her outfit anyway, she'd go all out.

She pulled out the flashiest dress, packed in case she got the chance to visit the theatre or to impress important people in the entertainment industry. It was a purple dress made from stretchable fabric with thousands of sequins sewn on it. She wriggled into the skintight dress and closed the back zipper before doing a swirl. Lacking a full-length mirror she looked down at herself, smoothing a wrinkle in the material here and there.

The dress felt smooth on her skin and left none of her curves to the imagination while still retaining her modesty. She adored the deep V-neck that enabled her to shrug off a strap and make her audience go wild with a bit of shoulder skin exposed. It was the perfect dress to turn heads and she'd worn it many nights on stage. In the beam of the spotlights it sparkled like a diamond but even in the dim light of this drab January morning, she wouldn't go unnoticed.

The thought of Otto's disapproving gaze amused her and she slid her feet into the matching silver heels before she repacked her suitcase. Once she was ready, she tossed her coat over one arm, took up the suitcase with the other hand and walked down the staircase like the star she was, prepared to make a grand entrance.

The smell of porridge grew with every step, but she wouldn't let such a mundane detail deter her. She just hoped they had real coffee to drink.

The bar was empty apart from Otto and Lutz sitting at a table eating breakfast. She strode inside, swaying her hips. Both men noticed her at the same time, but only one of them showed the usual reaction of a red-blooded male. Lutz's eyes all but popped out of his face and it was only when Maria appeared from the kitchen, with a bowl of porridge for Bruni, that he chastely lowered his gaze as if suddenly very interested in his breakfast.

Otto, though, wasn't impressed. Not a hint of desire appeared in his gaze as he gave her the once-over. Bruni wondered whether he did this for the sole purpose of taunting her. So far, he'd seemed completely immune to her sex appeal. While she certainly wasn't interested in the trucker, he could at least have had the grace to devour her with his eyes like every other man walking on this earth did.

Once he was finished with the perusal of her person, he finally showed a reaction. His voice was cold as ice as he said, "Have you completely lost your mind?"

"You don't like it?" She pushed one foot forward and bent her knee slightly, so that the front slit in the dress opened up and exposed her leg – clad in a fresh nylon stocking.

"I remember explicitly telling you to dress less flashy, and you show up with this...circus costume. If you haven't noticed, you're a passenger on a cargo truck and not on the *Titanic!*"

"I thought I'd spruce up your drab life with some glamour." A barely suppressed snort came from Maria as she walked around Bruni to set the bowl of porridge on the table and then stood behind her husband, putting a hand on his shoulder.

Oh, when would these glum housewives learn that their jealousy was misguided? Even before falling in love with Victor, Bruni had been extremely picky with her lovers and neither a trucker nor a garage owner would ever have made it into her bed.

"You will change into something more appropriate or you won't set foot in my truck again," Otto said and continued to spoon porridge into his mouth as if an order from him was somehow the law.

But she wouldn't be Bruni if she gave in. A little devil on her shoulder whispered into her ear, *Who does he think he is?* The only man who had permission to order her about was the stage manager at the cabaret, and she even defied him at times.

"Right here and now?" she said, with the sweetest smile.

"I don't care. As long as you're presentable when I'm done with my breakfast."

"And what exactly is not presentable about this dress?"

Maria nudged Lutz and both of them got up and silently walked into the kitchen, closing the door with a loud thud. Poor Lutz really didn't have much fun in his life.

"Everything," Otto said.

"Well, you will be disappointed then to learn that I didn't bring the dull apron you apparently expect a woman to wear."

His eyes flashed with anger, which wasn't the reaction she'd hoped for but she'd take it over his coldness any day of the week. There was a fine line between hate and love.

"Open your suitcase!"

"What?"

"I want to see for myself."

"Suit yourself." She put her suitcase onto the table and opened it for him. Let him get a hard-on while rummaging through her underwear.

He took one glance at the flashy dresses and matching heels, and asked, "What is this? Didn't you pack normal clothing?"

"No. I did not," she took great joy in telling him.

Otto cursed and slammed her suitcase shut. "Fine. But keep

your coat on, and closed, anytime we're not inside the truck. Got it?"

"If you wish." Her voice oozed honey. "Can I eat my breakfast now?"

"I'll wait in the truck. Departure in five minutes. Don't be late or I'll leave without you," he growled and left.

Bruni stared after him, her pride smarting from his lack of appreciation for her charms. She didn't know what was wrong with this man but she'd be damned if she'd give up trying.

The porridge was surprisingly good, but the coffee wasn't. If she ever needed one reason not to settle in the Soviet occupied zone, their lack of real coffee was more than enough.

Afraid that Otto would make good on his promise, she hurried up, yelled a "Thank you and good bye" into the kitchen and walked outside, where his truck stood in front of the entrance with the engine running.

She clambered in with some difficulty, and even before she was properly seated he pulled onto the road. They made good progress at first, until they hit a traffic jam. In front of them, a long line of vehicles moved at a snail's pace.

"Just great!" Otto banged his palms on the steering wheel.

"What's wrong?"

"Dunno. Could be an accident, a road closure, or simply a checkpoint."

"Are we close to the border yet?"

He snorted. "Not by a long way. And if this continues we won't get to Fulda before summer."

Her eyes opened in shock. That was six months away. He couldn't be serious. She'd be faster dancing all the damn distance. About an hour later they crawled up to a traffic control checkpoint.

"Don't say a word," Otto hissed. "Let me do all of the talking and keep your coat on."

She didn't share his opinion that the check would go more

smoothly if she covered herself up, but had no desire for a nasty argument with him. So she did as she was told, pushed her arms back into the sleeves of the coat and closed the front buttons.

The Soviet soldier approached the truck and extended his hand. "Papers."

Otto handed over his and Bruni's in his infuriatingly cool way as if he'd done this a thousand times. Which he probably had, given his line of work.

"What's your cargo?" the soldier asked, keeping their papers in his hands.

"The bill of lading is right here." Otto handed it over to him.

The man looked at it and stepped back. "Open up the rear, please."

Outwardly, Otto seemed to be completely calm, but Bruni sensed the tension rolling off of him in waves. He opened the driver's door and climbed from the cab, leaving her wondering what she should do. After a glimpse through the window at the slush outside she decided it was best to stay in the dry and warm truck.

Long seconds ticked away as she listened to the noises coming from the back. A rumble, voices, and finally the thud of a closing door. She let out the breath she'd been holding and plastered a smile on her face. A minute later, Otto showed up on the driver's side, his face frozen and fear lurking in his eyes. She opened her mouth to question him, but he made a quick motion with his hand to silence her.

"You will follow us to the next police station," the soldier said, his hand resting casually on his rifle.

Otto nodded his agreement and revved up the engine. Bruni waited until they were moving before she asked, "What happened?"

"They saw enough to know that I'm not just hauling furniture."

"And now? What will happen to us?"

"I don't know. Whatever they ask you, simply tell them you are from Berlin and paid me for a ride to Gotha." After a side glimpse at her, he added, "Tell them you were looking for work in a nightclub if they question your attire."

Very funny. As if she'd ever work in a C-class town like Gotha, where nobody had ever heard about a half-decent establishment. At least he seemed to be more honest than his tattoos made one assume, because he was telling her to save herself when he could very well have laid all the blame for the contraband on her.

Much too soon they arrived in the next town and stopped in front of the police station. Bruni was afraid of very few things, but now panic tingled up and down her spine.

CHAPTER 21

Victor was anxiously awaiting the doctor's verdict about when he was allowed to leave the hospital. Then he hoped to convince his superior to let him go to Berlin and see Bruni, before he was shipped home. For her, he would even get into one of those damned aircraft.

Time stood still and he was driving himself crazy with all the possible things the doctor might tell him, when finally the door opened and not one but three men in white coats entered the room.

"Lieutenant Richards," the head doctor said with a grave face. "We have done a few more tests and revised the x-rays again. The fractures in the tibia and fibula are healing just fine but we are worried about your knee."

"What's wrong with my knee?"

The second doctor chimed in, "See, the knee is a very complicated joint with ligaments, cartilage and bones. They must all work together to ensure the seamless movement and support of the body weight…"

Victor hoped the doctor would come to the point but he

continued with incomprehensible medical terms until Victor lost his patience. "What exactly does this mean for me?"

The three men looked at each other before the head doctor said, "I'm afraid your knee will stay stiff."

"Stiff?" Victor had difficulties wrapping his head around the news. "But I can still walk?"

"You can. With some training, the limp will be barely perceptible. But I'd say your time in the army is over. You'll be given a medical discharge."

"A medical discharge?" The fog in his brain thickened and he felt like a complete idiot.

"Yes. I'll fill out the paperwork and get it sent over to military command later today." The doctor gave a curt nod. "I know this comes as a surprise but I find these things are usually for the best. You'll see."

Victor watched the doctors leave, feeling like he was afloat on the ocean in a tiny lifeboat that was quickly losing air. He'd already been earmarked for demobilization, but a medical discharge? It was too much to bear for the moment.

People would think him a cripple and he'd have no job, no future, no nothing. And no Bruni. He could stay in Germany and try his luck as a civilian worker for the very army that wanted to discharge him because of a stiff knee. He closed his eyes and gasped as self-pity threatened to drown him.

The next morning, Glenn strode into the room, having found some time to visit between back-to-back flights to Berlin.

"Have you heard?" Victor asked.

"Did they find the driver?"

"No. And I still can't remember his face."

"What does the doctor say?"

"That my memory may, or may not, return. There's no way to tell and I should relax and not try to force it."

"Bah...I'd love nothing more than to wring that asshole's neck."

"Still having trouble with their antics?" Victor knew Glenn had been involved in a crash caused by a Soviet fighter plane buzzing him.

"Nah. Not since the crash. They seem to fear another war should they cause a fatal accident. I, for my part, would gladly drop a few bombs on the SMAD headquarters in Karlshorst."

"I'm sure you would." Victor's mood was finally lifting, until he remembered the words of the doctor. "Doc says my knee is never going to be fully functional again."

"But you'll still be able to walk?"

"Yes. But they're giving me a medical discharge. How horrible is that?"

Glenn stared at him, uncomprehending. "Eh? Haven't you asked for your demobilization papers already? So, what's the difference?"

"The difference is that I'm now officially a cripple."

"The morphine is messing with your head. Do you know how many men would switch places with you in a heartbeat?"

Victor grumbled something unintelligible, since Glenn was right but he still felt cheated out of his future.

"Did you deliver my letter to Bruni?"

"Not in person. They won't let us leave the plane, to ensure a faster turnaround. But I gave it to that buxom girl at the mobile snack bar in Tegel, along with a chocolate bar, and she promised to personally deliver it to Bruni's address."

"Thanks, man." Suddenly, Victor regretted not having given Bruni his parents' address back in the States, just in case.

"Sorry, but I need to get over to Zara's place or I'll be in deep trouble." Glenn's grin belied his words.

"Give her my greetings, will you? And if she hears from Bruni, let me know."

"I will. Although Zara officially doesn't know you're here."

"Oh yeah, I forgot. My stay here is top secret," he said bitterly.

CHAPTER 22

Otto followed the military car, pondering his options. Thanks to the cargo he'd blindly accepted, he was now in serious trouble. He cursed Heinz for foisting hot goods onto him, but also himself for not vetting his business contact more carefully.

He'd made it a principle to always stay on the gray side of the law. Running the blockade, yes, but only transporting legal stuff, like food or medicine. And now he was being escorted to a Soviet police station with a truckload of stolen antiques.

"It's not your fault," said Bruni, who'd been silent ever since the soldiers had ordered them to follow their car. Her words surprised him, since he could literally smell her disapproval and had wondered when she'd start verbally attacking him.

"But it is." He ran a hand through his hair.

"You got shafted."

"Because I was stupid. I should have dumped the stuff the moment you told me about it."

"Agreed, you were stupid, but only because you're a responsible man and no match for someone like Heinz, who'd sell his own grandmother for a good deal."

He looked at her, seeing a completely new side of the spoilt, high-maintenance nightmare she was. "Why are you dealing with him?"

"He's the Café de Paris owner's nephew, which is, without doubt, the best cabaret in all of Berlin. And..." she made an elegant gesture with her red varnished fingers, "...I'm, without doubt, the best singer in all of Berlin."

He broke out into laughter. "You're quite self-opinionated."

"I wouldn't be where I am if I weren't."

Otto looked at her again, getting the feeling there was so much more to her underneath the glamourous shell. He hadn't seen it– because she hadn't wanted him to see it. Just like the antiques, where he'd only seen the old furniture and not the precious items they actually were.

The car ahead turned left and came to a halt in front of a red brick building with the word *Polizei* painted above the door. They had arrived at the police station.

His palms became moist with sweat and, despite having done this a million times, he had difficulty in putting the truck in reverse to maneuver it into the parking spot the soldiers pointed at. Suddenly, he felt Bruni's small hand on his forearm.

"We'll talk our way out of it."

"I'd sure like to have your optimism." He somehow managed to park the truck. As soon as he opened the driver's door to climb down, he stared into the muzzle of a rifle. Bad memories from the war swamped him and, for a moment, he believed he was back in a trench. His vision blurred and all he could hear was shouting, explosions, and then silence.

"*Los, vorwärts!*" The soldier gave him a nudge with his rifle to emphasize the meaning of his words.

Otto blinked a few times, slowly returning to the present and stumbled forward, the disdain for Heinz, who'd put him in this situation, rising with every step. Without having to turn his head he knew Bruni was a few steps behind by the scent of her flowery perfume wafting into his nose. He heard the crunching of her ridiculously high, spiked heels on the gravel. He sure wasn't keen on her or her absurd attire, but there was no way he would abandon her to the likes of the Soviets.

Once they arrived at the reception desk, he and Bruni were separated and led into two different rooms. Much to his relief, the policeman in charge of his interrogation didn't seem interested in physical torture and merely asked questions.

"Is it true you're transporting stolen artworks?"

"No, I had no idea."

The policeman raised a brow. "Very unlikely."

"Please, you must believe me, I was shafted. My contact person told me I was to transport used furniture to Fulda."

"And it never occurred to you something might be fishy?"

"No. You have no idea what strange things people want transported. One time, a client wanted me to drive twenty stinking pigs—"

"You're right, I don't know and it doesn't interest me. So you claim your client lied to you?"

"Yes."

"His name?"

"Heinz."

"Heinz what?"

"I don't know his last name."

"Aha." The policeman made a note, looked at Otto with his brows drawn together and said, "He didn't give you his last name but it never occurred to you that this deal wasn't entirely legal?"

Otto grunted. The man had a point. Owning up might be his best defense. "Look, I admit, not everything I do is strictly legal. Sometimes I drive food into West Berlin. I was contracted to deliver the furniture as payment for a load of potatoes to pick up in Fulda."

"Aha."

"It never occurred to me that a load of potatoes might be worth more than a bunch of old furniture."

"We're talking about cultural heritage here. Art stolen by the fascists."

"I didn't know this. I'm a simple truck driver, I know nothing about art."

"Are you a fascist?"

"What? No! I'm an anti-fascist and love communism."

"Why do you work for the rotten imperialists then?"

"I don't. Never worked for an American, not since they mistreated me as a prisoner of war." The Americans had actually treated him quite well, but the policeman didn't have to know that. "I hate them as much as everyone else."

"And still you fell for their scam of a blockade and illegally transported food to Berlin that is sorely needed to feed the hard-working people in our zone?"

"I'm sorry, I just wanted to help."

"I don't believe a single word you've said." The policeman snapped his notepad shut and added, "And I don't actually care. The NKVD has been notified and they're on their way to fetch you and your little slut. Don't believe for one second they'll listen patiently to your lies the way I have."

He snapped his fingers and the door sprung open. A uniformed young man came in, applied cuffs to Otto's wrists and led him into a cell, where he took the cuffs off again and bolted the iron door.

Panic gripped Otto. Everyone knew how the NKVD worked – they were nothing but a crueler version of the feared Gestapo. He was afraid of very few things, but the NKVD torture dungeons were certainly one of them.

After a while, he heard the telltale toc-toc of Bruni's heels on the floor and his heart jumped with delight when the steps stopped in front of his cell and the door opened.

She strode inside, her purse clutched in her hand, her shoulders straight and her head held high as if she were about to go on stage, not be ushered into a cell. This woman truly was exceptional and it dawned on him that he'd severely underestimated her, judging her solely by her pretty face and stupid clothing.

She seemed not to notice him, because she walked over to the opposite wall and rested her forehead against the cold bricks. With her shoulders slumped forward, she looked so fragile, he couldn't resist feeling sorry for her and asked, "Are you okay?"

Despite her effort to look self-assured, he could see the fear in her eyes as she turned around. "Well…we were caught smuggling stolen antiques and are locked in a prison cell. So I guess okay wouldn't exactly describe it."

He bit back a smile. Had to give her credit for having guts. "I meant, did they hurt you in any way?"

"No, they didn't, but I'm fully confident the NKVD will, as soon as they have us in their clutches. The police believe we're holding back information on the instigators." She paused to inspect her nail. "It's chipped."

"What?"

"I chipped my nail and the oaf wouldn't even give me a nail file to fix it. Does he think I'm about to file my way through this iron door?"

Otto guffawed. "You really are one of a kind, lady. Who cares about a chipped nail when the NKVD is coming for you?"

"I do. Therefore, I think it best we leave this inhospitable place before they get a chance to chip another of my nails." Bruni was back to her haughty self, apparently unfazed by brick walls, locked steel doors, and armed soldiers.

"Got an extra set of cell keys hidden somewhere in that tight dress?"

"No, silly. As you would plainly see, if you bothered to look, there's no room to hide an extra piece of anything in this dress."

"So, what exactly is your great plan to get us out of here?"

She told him the rough sketch of her plan and he looked at her, shaking his head. "You're completely crazy. That will never work."

"We just need to wait for the perfect time, such as when all the policemen are out for lunch," she insisted.

Otto didn't comment, and Bruni pressed her lips together as if annoyed. After several seconds of silence, she pleaded, "Please. I can't do it without your help."

"You know that the chances of this working are slim."

"And, if we don't do it, the chances to get out unscathed are zero."

She had a point, although staging an escape attempt would suck them even deeper into trouble, making them hunted people. On the other hand...did he really want to find out whether the rumors about the NKVD were exaggerated?

"Fine. Let's do it."

CHAPTER 23

"It's time," Bruni whispered. "All the men bar one have left the building to go for lunch."

Otto nodded, but she could read in his expression that he wasn't at all comfortable with her plan. To tell the truth, she wasn't exactly confident herself, but she'd be damned if she'd sit here waiting for the Russians to torture her the way they had done with Zara. Bruni was no martyr; she'd prefer to be shot in the back while trying to escape than to endure what Zara had.

"*Zdraviya zhelauy samomou krasivomy ofitserou v gorode.*" Bruni opened the small window in the cell door and called into the hallway: *Greetings to the handsomest officer in town.* Her heart jumped with both joy and fear at once when the man turned to look at her. Her Russian was sketchy at best, but she had learned a few phrases from Feodor.

"What do you want?" He walked toward her with a suspicious gaze, his hand on his weapon.

"I need to pee, urgently."

He seemed unsure about whether to grant her request, so she added, "Please, *Privet soldatik*, I'll be forever grateful."

The man licked his lips at her endearment and said, "Alright, but I'll have to handcuff you."

"Whatever you want." Her voice was throaty.

"You'll stand two steps back from the door and this man stays in the corner, where I can see him."

"Understood." She stepped back and told Otto to stay in the corner. The policeman came to the door and peeked through the small window. When he saw that his orders were obeyed, she heard the clatter of keys and quickly rolled down the top of her stretchy dress.

He stepped inside and the hand holding his drawn pistol sank down as he stared, speechless, at her naked breasts. Bruni lasciviously licked her lips and Otto sprang into action, grabbing the pistol from the officer.

"Thanks, sweetie." Bruni took the key ring from him and left the cell. Otto kept the gun pointed at the Russian as he followed her. The top of her dress back in place, she locked the cell, leaving the key dangling in the lock, and dashed for the exit at the end of the hallway.

There was no time to waste, because they had no idea when the other policemen would return. Otto overtook her and hissed under his breath, "Meet me at the truck. I'll have the engine running."

Short of breath, she could only nod to show she understood. She had thought herself in good shape from singing and dancing all night on stage, but running even this short distance had her heaving like a locomotive. If her life hadn't been at stake, she'd have stopped and doubled over to catch her breath.

Her heels clicked on the tiled stone floor, the sound echoing off the walls and sending shivers of fright down her spine. When she reached the exit door she saw Otto rattling the truck's door handle and then he turned around with a gloomy expression.

He reached her halfway across the yard, took her elbow and said, "Damn Russians. Took the keys and locked the truck."

Turning in his direction, she wheezed, "Can't you pick the lock?"

"I could, but not quickly enough, especially because I also have to short-circuit the engine." His grip around her elbow tightened and he dragged her behind him at an impossible speed that had her more stumbling than running.

They crossed the street and went down an alley until they reached the border of the small town, where the pavement ended and a meadow began. Otto showed no mercy, dragging her behind him over rough and smooth. It was only thanks to his unforgiving grip that she even managed to stay upright. At times, though, she believed she'd never touch the earth again, as he drag-heaved her across yet another obstacle. Only when they reached the cover of the forest did he let her go.

Her heels kept sinking into the muddy earth and her tight skirt forced her to take small steps at a hurried pace. But the rascal didn't seem to care; he stormed ahead, apparently expecting her to follow with no hesitation.

Thoroughly out of breath, she collapsed onto a fallen log. Otto must have heard the thud, because he turned around, impatience written all over his face. She was too exhausted to speak, so she bent over in a slump, her heart hammering violently against her ribs. When she finally managed to sit upright her gaze fell on her favorite pair of heels, and she all but broke out in tears.

It took at least another minute before she'd caught her breath enough to speak. "Look at my shoes! I'm not walking a single step further!"

"Be my guest. Stay and wait for the Russians to capture you."

That threat was enough to scare the living daylights out of her and she struggled to get up. Otto extended his hand to help her, and for once she was grateful to have him by her side. That feeling lasted all of ten seconds, because while she finally found the time to close the zipper on her dress, he demanded, "Give me your shoes."

"What?"

"Now!"

Seeing the way his jaw tightened, she decided to indulge him, though it was a very bad time to take a closer look at her shoes. She took them off, one by one, in the most elegant manner she could manage while precariously balancing with her stockinged feet on the slippery log. "Here you go."

And what did the deplorable man do? He walked several steps to a large rock, bashed her precious shoes against it and broke the pointy heels off, turning them into what appeared to be flat-soled shoes.

"You...monstrous ruffian! Those were my favorite heels," Bruni screeched at him. "Do you have any idea how much they cost? They were a gift from the American Kommandant in Berlin and can't be purchased anywhere in Germany. He had them flown in for me from New York."

Otto tossed the ruined shoes back and nodded at her feet. "Put them back on. Frankly, I don't care how much they cost, how rare they are, or who bought them for you. All I care about is you being able to keep up with me."

"Feel free to walk ahead, if I'm too slow for you," she retorted, ignoring her sudden anxiety at the prospect of being alone in the forest. As a city girl, born and bred, she had little experience with nature and had never liked it, because, by definition, nature was dirty and Bruni hated dirt.

"I would, but I'm deeply indebted to you for saving my ass with that little stunt at the police station. You may have me pegged as a criminal, and you're right about that, but I do have an honor code, which means I'm not leaving you here to rot. Understood?"

She nodded, appreciating his honesty.

"It seems you haven't quite figured it out, so I'll spell it out for you: We are fugitives running from the Soviet occupying force... Got it?"

"Yes," she said ruefully. Her escape plan had ended after leaving the cell and she had no idea how to continue from here. For God's sake, she didn't even know where she was!

"Good. One more thing." He crouched in front of her, took the material of her dress into both hands and ripped the existing slit all the way up until it indecently showed off most of her thigh.

Bruni slapped at his hands. "What are you doing? Stop."

"Be quiet." He pulled the fabric until it tore just above her knees. "We'll be on the run for a while and you can't move fast enough in this crazy dress." He finished ripping the lower half of her skirt, looked at her and said, "Much better, but still not good."

"Am I supposed to be grateful you've ruined my shoes *and* my dress?"

"That would be nice, for starters." The infuriating man extended his hand, pulled her up and walked away.

She hurried to follow him in her mutilated shoes. It was a wobbly feeling to say the least and they were not at all comfortable or easy to walk in, but at least she didn't sink into the soft earth anymore. When she caught up with him, she asked, "Where are we going?"

"Away from here."

"Do you even know where we are?"

"As it happens, I have quite a good idea of our location. But before we can do anything else, we need to find you some practical clothes."

"And then what?" she asked, as they continued walking through the woods.

"Then we will see."

"How very reassuring," she mumbled under her breath.

CHAPTER 24

"Stay here and don't go anywhere. I'll be back as quick as I can."

"Where are you going?"

"To get you something more appropriate to wear." He glanced at her small frame and hoped he'd find something to fit her, although most anything would be better than that glitzy dress she was wearing. If he weren't scared shitless about the Russians capturing them, he'd laugh at how ridiculous Bruni looked traipsing through the forest. A fallen angel if there ever was one.

Without waiting for an objection he melted into the trees and approached the village a few hundred yards away. After the war, he'd sworn to change his ways and never steal again, but tough times required tough measures. Sure enough, he soon spotted what he was after. Looking left and right he snuck up to a line with freshly laundered clothes hanging out to dry.

A hen cackled and he froze, but nothing happened. He gazed around and broke into a satisfied grin when he noticed a pair of wellingtons standing next to the chicken coop. He took his time to observe the clothes softly wafting in the breeze and decided on a pair of rather smallish, dark blue overalls, which would blend in perfectly.

With three big strides he grabbed first the overalls and then the boots, and left the small farm seconds later like a ghost. In and out in seconds, that's how a good theft was done. He still had it in him.

"Well done," he congratulated himself and silently skulked back into the forest. The reflections of Bruni's glittery dress danced around the trees way before he spotted her.

"Thank God you're back," she said feebly when he stepped into her field of vision.

"You missed me?"

"Wouldn't you like that!" she retorted, but he noticed the relief in her eyes.

"Here. Put these on." He fully anticipated her scratching his eyes out when he offered her the new attire, but she merely gave him a disapproving glare. Still, that was better than expected.

"Where did you get those?"

"I'm pretty sure you don't want to know."

"You stole them." It was a statement. She looked at the overalls with a face as miserable as sin but got up and stretched out her hand to take them. "Turn around."

He complied and heard her slip off what was left of her dress to step into the dungarees. "You can look now."

"Now, that's a change." If they weren't alone in the woods he'd believe someone had switched the woman for another. The overalls had seemed small on the line, but were much too big for her. She'd rolled up the sleeves and stuffed the pant legs sloppily into the overlarge boots, but at least she now looked like any normal person.

"We'd better bury your old things," he said, making to dig a hole in the earth with his bare hands.

"They were perfectly new and fine before you ripped them apart."

"Okay, then let's bury your perfectly new, fine things."

"You…you…ruffian," she hissed in an exasperated tone, but threw her dress and shoes into the hole without further resistance.

He filled in the hole, adding a few leaves and twigs on top to disguise any traces of his work. "Let's go. We have a long walk ahead of us." He set a steady pace, making sure Bruni kept up with him. To give her credit, she never complained, but stoically trudged by his side, the large wellingtons squeaking with every step. At least they wouldn't have to worry about accidentally running into a wild boar or deer with all the noise she was making. After a while, they reached a road and he decided to walk alongside it, for faster progress.

"How much further do we have to go?" she asked, after several hours of hiking.

"Already tired of running away?" He motioned for her to sit down on the side of the road, since he felt sorry for her. Bruni looked a picture of misery, which was a stark contrast to the glamourous woman he'd picked up in Berlin.

"Honestly, I'm hungry, angry, frightened, sore, and at the end of my rope, but I'd never go back and risk being sent to one of their torture dungeons."

"They might not…"

"Or they might. And I'm not going to chance that." She removed her boots and wiggled her toes. Her nylon stockings had holes in them due to the harsh treatment, and her big toe stuck out. The color of the nail varnish matched that of her fingernails. She peered up at him, looking very vulnerable. "Thanks for escaping with me."

He was still torn between whether this had been a brilliant move or a horrible one, but he wouldn't let her see his doubts. "You're welcome."

"You may not understand why I was so hell-bent on getting out of there…but…my friend Zara was abducted by the NKVD, and I still wonder how she survived the ordeal. I wouldn't have. I'm not used to hardship."

"I barely noticed."

Bruni began to giggle, and the sound of her voice sent tingles down his spine.

"Your voice is exceptional, definitely on a par with Edith Piaf's." He'd admired the French singer ever since he'd heard her sing in Berlin during the war.

Bruni's eyes widened. "You know The Little Sparrow?"

"Not personally, but I'm a fan. She's by far the best entertainer in all of Europe. And her voice is to die for. She has such a wide tonal range, it's amazing. Whenever I listen to her songs, I get goosebumps all over."

"It's strange for a ...someone like you to say that."

"I always loved to sing, even attended the choir for a while."

"What happened?"

"Let's continue our walk and I'll tell you."

He extended his hand to help her up, but she only giggled. "First I have to put on these horrible boots again."

As they continued, he told her about his love for music and how that had received a big blow when his father had forbidden him to continue attending the choir, because it was unmanly.

"How ridiculous! On Christmas Day I attended a show by Bob Hope, and there's nothing unmanly about him. I would go so far as to suggest most of the women in the audience would have thrown themselves at his feet. And I'm pretty sure he took up more than one on the offer."

He didn't respond, since he had never slept with a woman, which Bruni wouldn't understand.

It was already dark when they came to the crossing he'd been watching out for. From here, it was only a two-hour hike or maybe three hours, with Bruni by his side, to his mother's house.

"We're almost there."

"Care to tell me where 'there' is?"

"Wittenberg."

"And what's in Wittenberg?"

"My mother's house. We'll arrive just before midnight, when all of the neighbors have gone to bed."

"Are you going to present me as your girlfriend?"

He cocked his head. His mother sure would love that. "If you don't mind being asked about grandkids."

"Really? Do I look like someone who wants to raise a bunch of kids?"

"Right now you look like a vagrant."

"Thanks to you. Remember that you threw away my perfectly fine dress for this?" She made a gesture down her body.

"It does give you an exotic appearance."

Bruni laughed at his remark and once again he realized that he'd completely misjudged her. When they reached the sleepy town of Wittenberg, he cautioned her to stay in the shadows as they made their way to his mother's house.

He knocked on the door, because his keys were still in the truck. It took several minutes until he heard scuffling steps and his mother calling out, "Who's there?"

"Mother, it's me. Otto."

She opened the door and immediately launched into a tirade. "What happened to your keys? Do you know what time it is? Waking your mother at this ungodly hour, you almost gave me a heart attack."

"I'm sorry, Mother. I've brought a friend, since we both need a place to stay for the night." He beckoned for Bruni to approach the door. "This is Bruni. And this is my mother, Frau Krause."

"Nice to meet you, Frau Krause. I'm very sorry for the inconvenience."

"Come in, come in." His mother stepped aside to let them

pass. She peered left and right, because he normally parked directly in front of the house. "Where's your truck?"

"That's a long story." He followed his mother into the kitchen.

"Are you hungry?" she asked, eying Bruni, who lingered in the background.

"Actually yes, the truck broke down and we haven't had the chance to eat dinner yet."

She furrowed her brows. "I hope it's nothing serious?"

"No, Mother, nothing that can't be fixed."

"Why don't you show your girlfriend where she can wash up, while I fix you something to eat?"

CHAPTER 25

B runi wasn't fooled by Frau Krause's friendly face. She couldn't blame the woman, because what mother would approve of her son bringing a shredded chicken in oversized men's overalls into her house? Certainly not anyone Bruni knew – or wanted to know.

"Come, I'll show you the bathroom." Otto rescued her from the awkward situation and directed her through a dust door into an adjacent tiled room with a toilet, a washbasin and an empty space with a barrel, a scoop, sponges, cloths and a piece of curd soap.

"Thank you." Even though she was bone-tired, she yearned to wash the grime off of her skin. One glimpse into the mirror and she recoiled from the hideous woman staring back at her. Her makeup smudged, dirt smeared across her face from falling several times, her hair a tangled mess – no wonder Otto's mother had cast a disapproving gaze at her.

She stepped next to the barrel, ladled cold water over her body and furiously scrubbed off the evidence of her day from hell. The curd soap left her delicate skin reddened, but she barely noticed the sting, so relieved was she to be clean again.

Last, she dunked her head into the water barrel to wash her hair, without soap since it would only entangle her dyed curls.

If she'd been in her own home, she would have wrapped a towel around her body and another one around her head, but here she stared with disgust at the dirty overalls she would have to put on again. As she stood naked, relishing that precious feeling of being freshly washed, she heard muffled voices from the kitchen. Curiously, she inched closer to the door to eavesdrop.

"When I suggested you go and find a nice girl to marry, I didn't expect you to search in the woods for the most ragged vagrant possible."

"Mother, please. I told you the truck broke down and we had a rough day."

"A rough day? You and that tramp all day in the woods? By the looks of it you did a lot of rolling around."

Otto didn't respond. It reminded her of her childhood, when her own mother had scolded Bruni for the things her father had done to her. She shrugged it off. Those days were long gone, and these days she called the shots in her life. Although, right now, she felt almost as helpless as back then. And her reaction had been the same, too: running away.

It didn't matter whether she was running from an abusive father or the Soviets; she'd managed once before and she would manage again, with or without Otto's help. And she'd not let the scathing words of his mother make her feel inadequate, in any way at all. She was Bruni von Sinnen, the popular entertainer, for God's sake!

She stepped back, put on the overalls once more and opened the door extra loudly on purpose. As much as she'd love to give his mother the silent treatment for her insult, she was much too hungry to put that plan into action. She hadn't learned to smile through her tears for nothing and, soon enough, the sun would shine again when she came out the other side.

A short time later, she sat at the kitchen table silently spooning up a hearty potato soup with bread, while listening to Otto and his mother converse. It seemed his mother was aware of, and very opposed to, his smuggling ways.

Bruni ate as quickly as she could, and said, "Thank you, Frau Krause, for the meal. I would like to be excused now as I'm very tired."

Otto jumped up. "I'll show you where you can sleep."

She followed him up the steep stairs into a tiny room that still featured remnants of his childhood, among them a huge stuffed bear and a few photos of him in the Hitler Youth uniform. The only pieces of furniture were a single bed nestled against the wall and a battered dresser with the drawer fronts falling off.

"You can have the bed and I'll sleep on the floor," he offered, as he turned on a lamp. "We need to leave first thing in the morning."

"Where are we going?" Bruni asked, as she wandered over to the bed and sat down on the edge, took off her boots and put them on the floor.

"I'll get you to the border, somehow. Do you need anything else?" he asked, as he moved toward the door.

"No. Thank you."

"Get some sleep. I'll be back in a bit." Otto left the room, obviously to give her the privacy to undress and slip beneath the covers before he returned to sleep on the floor.

It was a considerate gesture, although she wouldn't have minded sharing the bed with him to warm her up, as long as he kept his hands to himself. And if not, she had learned ways to thwart unwanted groping. She wasn't a helpless child anymore.

CHAPTER 26

P ulling the door shut behind him, Otto walked to the top of the stairs and listened to the sounds of his mother moving about in the kitchen. He knew she was waiting for him to return. He found her washing the dishes.

"Let me help you," he said, and took up the tea towel.

"Since when do you help without me having to beg you?"

He ignored the snide remark and waited for her to talk, since he could see in her face how unhappy she was about Bruni's presence.

"Is your lady friend sleeping?"

"She's working on it. By the way, I might need to disappear for a while."

She looked at him with concern, slowly shaking her head. "Will the sorrow you bring me never end?"

"I'm not intentionally trying to cause you pain." He and she didn't see eye to eye on many things but he still loved her. After his father's death he'd become rebellious – a trait not appreciated in Hitler's Reich – and had served several prison terms. Mostly for petty theft or defying the authorities in other ways.

Otto simply wasn't cut out to obey orders he found stupid,

unjust, or downright cruel, not back then and sure as hell not now. Regardless of how justified his insubordination had been, each time he'd gotten into trouble it had hurt his mother.

"Who is after you?"

"The Soviets. The last cargo didn't go the way I planned."

"Why do you even have to undertake these illegal trips into West Berlin? You need to stop going rogue and become a law-abiding citizen."

It wouldn't do any good to tell his mother that the Soviets were the bad guys and the entire chokehold on Berlin was illegal – and a million times more damaging than him helping to keep civilians fed.

"And do what? I'm making good money with these runs, and you well know that we need it." As if to prove the truth of his words, she was shaken by a coughing fit. The doctor had diagnosed severe bronchitis, possibly caused by the air pollution due to everyone heating with brown coal. He gave her cough syrup but what she really needed were antibiotics and an extended stay at the seaside – both things they couldn't afford.

"They are always looking for workers at the nitrate factory. And the people there make good money in addition to getting extra ration cards."

"You need to be a member of the communist party to get a job there," he reminded her. It was a sore spot between them. During his youth he'd sympathized with the ideas of the communists, had even admired them for having the guts to stand up against Hitler but, after the war, those very same communists had adopted the Nazi playbook and used each and every detail, albeit with different titles.

"So why don't you join? I did months ago."

It was typical of his mother to follow the new leaders without question but he hadn't let them cajole him into joining the NSDAP back then, and for the same reason he wouldn't join the SED now. It was just another way to force some stupid ideology on unsuspecting citizens and bring them to heel. Thank you very much but no thanks.

"They probably wouldn't even accept me because of my previous convictions."

"And there you are wrong," she said, with a triumphant expression on her face. "First, those convictions happened under the Nazis and they will only serve to prove that you opposed them when nobody else dared. Second, the communists actually care about their citizens and if you go to the party office and tell them you regret being a nuisance and promise not to continue whatever shady stuff you are doing, they'll give you a second chance."

He sincerely doubted that and was sure the communists would, sooner or later, use it against him if he even so much as hinted at any wrongdoing. He'd seen it happen often enough to know that formerly well-accepted people were thrown into prison to disappear without a trace until Nevermas. "I will do that. But first I need to disappear for a while until the fuss dies down. If anyone asks, tell them you haven't seen me since last week."

Her lips thinned into a barely visible line. "I hope you know what you're doing, Otto Krause."

"I do." He kissed her cheek. "I'd better get some sleep now."

CHAPTER 27

Heavy pounding downstairs jolted Bruni awake. Within seconds, fear raced through her veins like a burning liquid. Before she even knew what was happening, Otto rose fully dressed from his makeshift bed on the floor and tossed her the overalls and boots.

"Get dressed. Fast," he whispered, pulling on his boots. She was still struggling with her clothing when he motioned for her to be quiet and pushed the window ajar.

The pounding became louder and she heard a male voice shout, "Open up!"

Otto grabbed two woolen sweaters from a drawer, motioned for her to put one on and to come to the window. She really hoped she was misinterpreting his plans.

His mother stomped down the stairs and yelled, "What the hell is happening? Do you have any idea of the time?"

"We are looking for your son, Otto Krause. Is he here?"

"I haven't seen him in a week. His truck isn't parked outside, so I'm sure he didn't come home last night."

"We found the truck but not him."

"I hope nothing bad happened to him! He's always doing

these dangerous runs, all alone, sleeping in his truck overnight. Do you think he's injured?"

Meanwhile, Bruni had her boots on and had shrugged into the overlarge pullover. Otto fully opened the window. The night was crisp and clear, and she easily heard the conversation between his mother and the soldiers.

"We still need to search your house."

"Of course, officer. I'm a good communist with nothing to hide. I joined the party months ago, although they wouldn't let me hold an office because of my frail health."

"Open the door."

"Just let me get this chain off. It sticks sometimes," his mother shouted. She finally got the chain loose and invited the soldiers in.

The moment Bruni heard their steps inside the hallway, Otto slid out of the window and onto the roof, holding out his hand toward her.

You've gotta be kidding me. For a split-second, she considered staying and resigning herself to her fate, but then the fighting spirit took over and she grabbed his hand. If she had to die she'd prefer a quick fall from a roof to being slowly tortured to death. As soon as she heard heavy boots stomping up the stairs, she hurriedly stuck one leg out of the window, and then the other, refusing to look down, all while she squeezed Otto's hand tight.

"Careful, but we need to hurry," he whispered, and pulled her behind him across the roof, stopping when they came to the edge. The way he moved showed this wasn't the first time he'd used the route, but for Bruni it definitely was.

She stared down at the ground, dimly lit by the half moon, and pondered whether she'd survive a calculated jump or not. Otto, though, didn't give her time to think, because he stepped across the short distance to the next house and tugged at her hand to follow him.

On the other side she barely believed she'd actually done it.

Once again, Otto gave her no time to pause, pulling her at a hazardous speed across rooftops, using steps intended for the chimney sweeper to climb up, then sliding down on their bottoms on the other side, thus moving from house to house.

It all happened with such speed that Bruni never fully comprehended her actions until they reached the end of the street, and Otto let her hand go. "Now we have to jump."

"From the roof?" Her loud whisper was shrill. She winced, hoping nobody had heard it.

"It's only the second floor, and I'll catch you." His words had barely registered, before he'd jumped down, and – much to her surprise – quickly straightened himself and turned to raise his hands toward her.

Come on, Bruni. You can't stay on the roof. She closed her eyes – and jumped. Miraculously, she landed safely in his arms, and he set her down on the soft grass. Looking at her sturdy wellingtons, she was grateful he'd forced her to wear them, as well as the dark blue overalls. Her purple sequin dress would have glowed like a walking lightbulb, enabling anyone to spot her from miles away. But then, she'd never anticipated being forced to run from Soviet military police after being accused of smuggling stolen artwork.

As soon as Otto let her go her wobbly knees gave out beneath her. Never the athletic one, the exertion and excitement had been too much and she huddled on the ground, shivering like aspen leaves.

"Get up, we need to find a safe place to stay."

"I can't," Bruni said, close to tears.

"You can and you will." He took both her hands and yanked her to her feet; nevertheless Bruni was too shocked to move. Suddenly, she felt a stinging slap on her cheek, which snapped her out of her stupor. Before she could protest, Otto said, "Sorry about that, but we really need to get going. They might still be looking for us."

She stared wide-eyed, unable to form a coherent thought, but her legs somehow moved all by themselves when he took her hand and pulled her behind him. They ventured through dark backstreets until they reached the main road leading out of Wittenberg. Otto crossed the road and led them into the cover of the wooded area running parallel to the road.

He seemed so sure of himself, knowing where to go and what to do, whereas she stumbled over sticks and rocks in her path. After some time, she stopped counting how often she fell, picked herself up again and pushed forward. It was as if her entire life consisted of nothing but walking.

When she'd paid Heinz to help get her out of Berlin and into the American zone, she'd believed it would be a matter of a day or two at most until she saw Victor again, but with every step she took in the dark forest, this goal seemed to get further out of her reach.

CHAPTER 28

Otto needed a plan. Walking through the nighted forest, he realized with sudden clarity that he couldn't return home for a long time, since the Soviets wouldn't miraculously go away and neither would his arrest warrant. He needed a place to hunker down for several weeks or months until it was all water under the bridge. His mother would be out of her mind with worry, he knew that, but she'd cope, as she always had.

His priority, though, was to get Bruni to the inner German border, and for that he needed a car. They would never arrive, if they had to travel all of the two-hundred-something miles on foot. A familiar face came to mind and a surge of renewed energy pushed him forward.

"I have an idea where we can go." He almost laughed out loud at the way Bruni's eyes lit up with unabashed hope.

"Someone who can help us?"

"Yes." He wasn't one-hundred-percent sure, but he was betting on the fact that Felix still had fond feelings for him and wouldn't send him away in his time of need. Under different circumstances, in a more tolerant world, the two of them might still be a couple and living happily ever after.

"How much longer?"

"Just around the corner."

She giggled. "I don't believe a single word you say."

"Okay, it's less than five miles from here and we should arrive before sunrise. There we can get some sleep and make further plans."

They trudged forward, Otto always hurrying her on, because he absolutely wanted to arrive at Felix's place before the day arrived. Finally, the village came in sight and he headed straight for his favorite watering hole. Knocking on the backdoor, he prayed Felix would welcome them in.

"Who's there?"

"It's me, Otto."

Seconds later, a tall and slim man with dark hair opened the door. "Otto, you here at this hour?" he asked, stepping forward to pull him into a bear hug.

Otto hugged him back, closing his eyes as he absorbed the embrace. Although he visited Felix's bar regularly, they always made sure never to be alone in each other's company so as not to be tempted to kindle the fire of their passion.

"And who's this lady?" Felix asked with a raised brow at the sight of Bruni standing two steps behind.

"Felix, this is Bruni. Bruni, my friend Felix."

"Nice to meet you," she said in her melodious voice, as if it was the most natural thing in the world to show up ragged and tired at the backdoor of a bar.

"Same." Felix turned back to Otto with a look of concern. "Why don't you come in, before someone sees you?"

Felix was no stranger to fistfighting patrons in his waterhole that catered primarily to the male workforce, and it didn't need a genius to see that Otto and Bruni were in dire trouble.

They followed him inside through a small hallway, past the

stockroom, the kitchen, and into the deserted bar, which was cast in twilight by the rising sun. All the chairs were up on the tables and, as was his custom, Felix had swept the floor clean after the evening's last guest had left.

"Sorry to wake you this early." Otto felt a twinge of guilt.

"Not a problem for me, but I guess it is for you."

"Right. I'll tell you everything over a cup of coffee."

"Always in need of a coffee." Felix chuckled. "You want one too, Bruni?"

"Yes, please. I could certainly use one."

Felix busied himself making coffee in the kitchen and when he returned several minutes later with three mugs in his hands, he said, "Otto, switch on the light behind the bar, will you?"

He placed the mugs on the counter and turned around to hand one to Bruni, when his eyes shot wide open. "Tell me it's not true."

"Excuse me?"

"You're the girl from the newspaper."

Bruni gave a proud smile before she seemed to realize that this might not be such good news as it seemed.

Otto frowned. "What newspaper?"

"This." Felix slid a copy of *Neues Deuschland* across the bar top toward him. On the front page was a picture of Bruni in her cream dress holding an invisible microphone in her hand. The headline read, "Vicious traitor and smuggler of our cultural heritage". The article went on to explain how she and her accomplice, a trucker called Otto Krause, had been caught robbing the German workers and farmers of valuable art to sell to the imperialist West.

"Oh...my...God," Bruni whispered.

"Didn't I tell you to keep a low profile? Look what you've done! It's all your fault!" Otto burst out. Her recklessness had just quashed their chances of ever returning to a normal life again.

"Is it, now?" She rose up on her bar stool, her feet on the pole running along the counter base, which made her the same height as Otto. "If I had known you were smuggling hot goods, I would never have put a foot into that awful truck of yours."

"What did you expect? None of the haughty, self-righteous men you usually associate with dared to take the risk and smuggle you out of Berlin. So don't put the blame on me, you knew exactly what you were getting yourself into."

Felix's jaw sagged more with every sentence, his eyes jumping between the two of them. Otto cast him an angry glare, but the longtime barkeeper knew when to jump into a brawl and when not. Apparently, for now, he found it more interesting to hear them accuse each other.

"I never signed up to being arrested and having to escape prison," she hurled at Otto.

"Then you shouldn't have played the big star in that bar."

"Or maybe you shouldn't have smuggled antiques."

"So it's true?" Felix interrupted their quarrel and both heads turned toward him.

"Unfortunately, it is. I was tricked," Otto admitted, running a hand through his hair. "I was told to take a load of furniture to Fulda but turns out there were valuable paintings, antiques, and whatnot hidden between."

"Which you would have noticed had you as much as glimpsed into the back of your truck before driving off," Bruni quipped.

"I did check the cargo, but not everyone lives a fancy life of privilege as you and has knowledge about the finer arts." Otto struggled to keep his voice down. If she were a man, she would have gotten a taste of his fists by now.

"You think you know it all, don't you? Just because I have managed to pull myself up by my bootstraps doesn't mean I've always enjoyed a good life. On the contrary, if you knew anything about my childhood you'd be weeping by now."

Before Otto could retort, Felix put a hand on his shoulder and said, "That's enough. The two of you are deep in the mire."

"I know." Otto let his forehead fall on the counter with a loud thud.

"The article offered a bounty for tips leading to your arrest. You're lucky there's no image of you in the paper, Otto, or the police would already be swarming this place."

"They almost caught us at my mother's house," groaned Otto. "We came to you because we need a car to cross the border into the American zone."

"You know I would give you my car in a heartbeat, but with this…" Felix tapped the newspaper. "I can't. They'll have traffic controls everywhere and will catch you even before you reach the next city. You can't even refuel somewhere without risking that someone will call the police."

"For a juicy reward, most everyone would be willing to sell us out."

"You can't trust anyone, not even your friends," Felix said.

"Not even you?"

"I would never betray you voluntarily, you know that. Although I can't guarantee anything if the Soviets decide to bring out the pilliwinks."

A shiver ran down Otto's spine. If the Soviets found out there had been more than friendship between the two men, they'd use a lot worse than thumbscrews on Felix.

Bruni, who had been remarkably silent during their conversation, piped up, "We could take a train, maybe?"

Otto shook his head. "Too dangerous. Even if Felix buys the tickets, we'll still have to get past the conductor, who may or may not check our papers. Especially when he recognizes your very distinguishable platinum blonde curls."

"Wait…" His expression pensive, Felix put up a hand. After several seconds a grin flickered across his face. "Remember how we used to get to the city when we were still at school?"

"Nah…she won't make it."

Bruni gave him the evil eye. "What do you assume I'm not capable of doing?"

"Train hopping," Felix and Otto said in unison.

"Of course I'm capable." Her voice sounded confident, but Otto saw the glimmer of fear in her eyes. Although what choice did she have? Staying in the Soviet occupied zone would lead to her capture sooner or later.

"You'll get as far as Eisenach without too much trouble. And from there it's not far to the border."

"How far, exactly, is not far?" Bruni asked.

"Maybe fifteen miles, more or less."

She groaned. "But they'll still arrest us as soon as they check our papers."

Another sly grin formed on Felix's face. "That's why you shan't show them your papers."

Otto knew what his friend was thinking. Felix might have become a respectable bar owner, but that didn't mean he'd forgotten about his former, less legal, life. "You mean the green border?"

"Yep. Only problem is how to cross the Werra river."

"We can't possibly swim over."

"No. And that's the biggest risk on your journey. You need to take to the road and cross on one of the bridges."

Otto finally took a sip of his coffee. "They know we're headed for Fulda, so maybe it would be better to cross farther north?"

"Hmm…if the Soviets are clever, they'll have control posts on every bridge near the border between Eisenach and Salzwedel."

"What if we go east instead?" Otto mused.

"East? Into Poland? That's flat-out crazy," Bruni groused.

"Not necessarily. We could travel by train all the way down

to the Czechoslovakian border and at the last moment divert to cross into the American sector via the Thuringian Highland."

"Where exactly is that?" Bruni asked.

"In the southeastern part of the Soviet zone, bordering both Czechoslovakia to the east and the American zone to the south. The Soviets will never in their wildest dreams expect us to head east."

"It could work," Felix said. "There's not much down there apart from sparsely-populated forest."

Bruni's face took on a peculiar look at the mention of forest.

"Then it's a plan." Otto finished his coffee. "Can we sleep here until evening?"

"Sure. Do you have money?"

"I do," Bruni said.

"You do? But where?" Otto gazed at her in disbelief, because she'd had to leave both her suitcase and purse in Soviet custody.

"Right here." She patted the triangle between her legs.

Felix broke into laughter. "Your spoilt hoity-toity lady may not be as useless as we both thought."

"It never pays to underestimate me. And if you're wondering whether I have enough, I also have this…" She pushed her hair behind her ears and exposed two golden ear studs.

With everything settled, Felix led them to his private rooms above the bar to sleep and promised to wake them in the afternoon when it was time to walk to the train station, to try hitching a ride on one of the freight trains passing through.

CHAPTER 29

Despite knowing it was next to impossible, Victor still hoped he'd somehow hear from Bruni. He hadn't been able to give his location in the letter, but since she was an intelligent woman, she'd figure it out.

Even if she didn't, he banked on the fact that she would somehow get in touch with Glenn or Zara to relay a message to him. But nothing happened. Day after day trickled by and he still hadn't heard a peep from her.

This morning, at an hour she usually drank her morning coffee and read a newspaper, he had wheeled himself to the payphone in the reception area and called her. But nobody had answered the phone.

Exhausted from the exertion, he collapsed on the bed, brooding over her extended silence. Others might consider this normal, but knowing Bruni he was dead certain something was amiss. She didn't care about rules and wouldn't be deterred just because it was forbidden to contact him.

On the contrary, he believed she'd move heaven and earth to find out where he was. So, what was the problem? A horrifying thought crossed his mind. What if the Soviets had abducted her to get to him? It was farfetched, to say the least, but he wouldn't put anything past the vile scumbags. Someone who was allegedly capable of organizing an assassination attempt on him was also capable of harming Bruni.

The thought made his stomach churn and, if he'd been able to walk, he would have raced from the hospital and back to Berlin, no matter who or what told him not to.

The door opened and Glenn breezed into the hospital room with his usual carefree attitude. "Hey man, how are the nurses treating you?"

"Torturing me with their physical exercises."

"I heard you might be getting out of here soon."

"That's what they tell me. But I'm under strict bedrest even then."

"I can think of worse," Glenn said with a salacious grin, although after falling in love with Zara, Glenn was all talk and didn't live up to his reputation as a womanizer anymore.

"Not without Bruni by my side."

"About her...Zara got a letter from Marlene."

"What does she say? Is Bruni okay?"

"So here's the thing." Glenn sat on the edge of his bed. "She's asking whether Bruni arrived safely."

"Where?"

"Here."

"Here? Why?"

Glenn tapped a finger on his forehead. "Did the accident damage your brain? To see you, obviously."

Glenn might be right, because Victor's brain *was* slow to work. "But she doesn't know where I am, so why would she come here? And how? Doesn't the blockade impede West Berliners from traveling to the other zones?"

"If you'd let me finish..."

"Okay. My mouth is shut."

"Understandably, Zara was super worried and finally

managed to telephone Marlene. And here's the crazy stuff: Bruni left Berlin almost two weeks ago. She arranged a ride with one of the blockade running truckers going back and forth between the Soviet zone and Berlin."

"Two weeks?" Victor asked, barely able to breathe out of worry for his fiancée. "It takes two days at most to get here."

"That's what Zara said, too."

"Do you think she got hurt? An accident? Maybe the Soviets arrested her to get to me?" Victor felt as if the blood in his veins was freezing over.

"No. We would have heard of anything like that by now, but I'm afraid you must come to grips with another possibility."

Victor eyed Glenn with suspicion, wondering what on earth he could mean with that cryptic phrase. "And that would be?"

"Don't shoot me. I'm just the messenger."

"Look at me, do you think I'm able to shoot anyone?" Victor rolled his eyes. In his current immobile condition he wasn't a danger to anyone, even if he'd somehow had access to his service weapon.

"Zara was pretty surprised when she first heard about you and Bruni. She didn't think Bruni was capable of loving anyone but herself. And then you guys went and fell head over heels."

"Bruni fought me every damn inch of the way, but she had no chance." Victor grinned, remembering how he'd courted her from the moment he'd first seen her on stage, singing *I'm in the Mood for Love*. Probably every man in the audience had assumed the same, but Victor knew it was him her gaze had been riveted to throughout the song.

"I mean, maybe you and Bruni have different expectations about this relationship."

"What are you talking about?"

"Has it ever occurred to you that she used you to get out of Germany?"

"Never."

"You wouldn't be the first one."

"Bruni has many flaws, but lying and pretending isn't one of them."

"But she is known to always look out for her own benefit in everything she does."

Victor sat up in his bed. He remembered Bruni saying that very thing herself. Multiple times. She'd been very clear upfront what her requirements for a relationship were, and that he didn't fulfill them, since he had neither the rank nor the spending power to keep her in the lifestyle she wanted. But she had changed, had admitted to falling in love with him. "She truly loves me. Why else would she embark on a dangerous trip through the Soviet zone to come and visit me?"

"So, if she loves you so much, why hasn't she arrived yet?"

Before Victor could answer, a nurse peeked inside. On seeing Glenn, she said, "I'm sorry, sir, but you'll have to leave now. Visiting hours are over."

"I'll come to see you again when my schedule permits." Glenn waved and left Victor to his thoughts.

Like everyone else, Glenn was fooled by Bruni's pretty face, didn't know what she had endured to become so cynical, and would never understand that their love for each other was pure.

In the afternoon, Victor took to his wheelchair and wheeled himself to the water cooler in search of company to keep his mind off worrying about Bruni's safety.

It was the first time he'd ventured this far, and he was sweating profusely from the exercise when he reached the sad group of patched-up servicemen, most of them aircrew who'd survived a rough landing, but also several ground crew who'd tested the endurance of their bones against spare parts or laden crates. Three of them were sitting around a table with two dice on top.

"Playing craps?" Victor asked, about the popular betting game.

"Wanna join us?" said one of the soldiers with a bandaged head.

"Would love to, I've been bored to death."

"You new here?"

"Not really, been in here for close to three weeks now, but this is the first time I've ventured this far."

"Looks pretty awful. Crashed your bird?"

Victor felt slightly ashamed, since his accident hadn't happened while on duty, but after a night out on the town. "Actually, it was a hit-and-run accident."

"What, here? Who'd do that? I mean, the civilians don't even have cars."

Mindful of the warning that he wasn't to tell anyone his whereabouts, he decided not to give further explanations. "I'm Victor, by the way."

He joined in their game of craps but his mind was elsewhere and, after a while, he excused himself and pushed his wheelchair over to the large windows, from where he could overlook the airfield with the ascending and landing planes. He missed his work, the damn field of dirt called Tegel airport. Heck, he even missed the crazy, oppressive atmosphere in Berlin. And he missed Bruni like a detached limb.

Remnants of snow lay in the protective shadows of the buildings, but the sun shone bright in the sky and soon the days would start getting longer and spring would arrive. He wouldn't be around to see it, because by then he'd already have returned to the States.

A sharp pain seared his heart. He absolutely had to apply for a marriage license beforehand, otherwise he might never see Bruni again. Caught in his thoughts about her, his ears perked up when two men a few feet away mentioned a cabaret singer who'd disappeared from Berlin.

"...can you imagine? That woman has completely vanished. I wonder if the Soviets are behind it?"

"Are they still abducting people?"

"Not in our sector, but this one worked and lived in the French sector, and you know how good the French are at keeping law and order." They both guffawed.

Victor, though, needed to get to the bottom of this and wheeled himself over to their table. "Sorry to interrupt, but would you know her name, by any chance?"

"Nah. Never saw her on stage myself, since I arrived late to the game when they wouldn't let us leave the plane to venture into town."

"Are you talking about that singer from Berlin?" A nurse with a cigarette in one hand and a cup of coffee in the other one came over.

"Yes." Victor looked at her, eager to get some news.

"Her name is something von Sinnen. It's a mad story about a crazy woman." She looked around before focusing on Victor, who was enraptured by what she had to say. "Her disappearance is making waves. One day, she simply didn't show up for work and naturally everyone assumed the Russians had abducted her, but no..." her voice dropped to a discreet whisper "...turns out she fell in love with a truck driver. And not just anyone, but a criminal. So, this German Bonnie and Clyde got arrested for smuggling..." She paused for impact and looked at the small group of patients who'd gathered, eager to relieve their boredom by hearing the newest gossip.

"...art stolen by the Nazis. And this is huge. Apparently, there's a criminal ring smuggling antiques, paintings, tapestries, and anything valuable, out of Berlin to sell to rich individuals, mostly in the States. It seems the artifacts that were found by the Soviets had previously been requisitioned from museums all over Europe by the Nazis."

"How do you know all this?" Victor asked.

"I have a relative in the Soviet zone and she sometimes sends me newspaper snippets with her letters, to show me proof of how benevolent the Russians are and how they care for the ordinary people. Not that I believe any of that crap." She took a drag and slowly exhaled the smoke.

Victor was on tenterhooks to find out what else she knew about Bruni. "So, that singer, she's in prison now?"

"She was. But the pair broke out."

"They broke out? Two Germans getting away from Soviet military police? We should cheer for them," one soldier said.

"They're still criminals," the nurse answered. "Although, apparently they claimed someone had set them up. But instead of working with the authorities to solve the case, they escaped."

"Can't hold that against them. Working with the Soviets will only get you deeper into trouble. We all know that," the man with a bandage around his head said.

"Anyway, the lovebirds ran off and the Russians haven't been able to catch them. They have vanished without a trace. Rumor has it they eloped and have been seen en route to Switzerland with a coffer full of money."

"That can't be true..." Victor protested weakly, before he shut his mouth. It wouldn't do to let his compatriots know that the *German Bonnie Parker* was his fiancée.

"Who knows? Fact is, the Soviets haven't been able to find them." She looked at the clock on the wall. "Sorry, I need to go back to work."

Victor wheeled back to the window overlooking the airfield. Despite his irrational fear of flying, he wished he could get up and hitch a ride in one of the aircraft going to Berlin. What that nurse had just said was utter bull. Bruni wasn't a criminal. She was an opportunist, calculating, cynical, but never a smuggler and certainly not someone who would elope with a truck driver.

How many points would a trucker score on her "ideal boyfriend" list? If he was good-looking, maybe one out of ten.

She'd not even wanted to go out with Victor that first time because he didn't have enough chevrons on his shoulder.

But at the same time as he dismissed the idea, he visualized pictures of Bruni entangled in the arms of another man and he wanted to scream with jealousy. No, she would not. Never. She was loyal. Perhaps not in the conventional meaning of the word, but she would never betray a friend. And he considered himself not only her lover, but also her friend.

As soon as he brushed the image away another one surged into his mind: of Bruni wearing a tight dress and impossibly high heels. He laughed out loud at the notion of her literally running in those shoes. The entire story was devoid of even a germ of truth.

Only…what had happened to her then? He gave a frustrated groan. Held captive in a wheelchair, he was unable to investigate.

CHAPTER 30

Bruni pondered when exactly her luxurious life had turned into a trip to hell. Was it when Victor had been injured? When she'd hatched the plan to travel to Wiesbaden in his pursuit? Or when she'd set foot into Otto's truck? When they had been arrested by Soviet police? Or rather, when she'd daringly escaped from prison? Or…when she'd agreed to this absolutely debasing activity called train hopping?

There'd been so many junctions in her life during the past months and apparently each and every decision she'd taken had only thrown her deeper into the mud. She was so sick and tired of living like a hobo and yearned to be back in her old life in Berlin.

Finally, she came to the conclusion that the disaster had run its course from the moment she'd first met Victor in the Café de Paris. A dreamy smile came to her face as she vividly remembered that evening: she was launching into her most popular song, *I'm in the Mood for Love*, when she spotted him watching her, mesmerized. Which wasn't unusual per se, but somehow, this tall, broad-shouldered man with the dirty blond hair, the green-gray eyes, and the devastating smile had caused her heart to flutter from the very first moment she'd set eyes on him.

Not one to succumb to the romanticized idea of love, because it was a concept used by the patriarchy to subdue women into sacrificing their ambitions for men, she'd fought Victor – and her feelings for him – tooth and nail, until...until she'd realized he was different. His love for her wasn't patronizing or oppressive, and neither was it abusive or manipulative. With him she always felt like she was not alone in this world.

He looked out for her, cared for her, cherished her. Not because he wanted her body for himself, or her beauty to impress business partners, or whatever other motives men usually had. But because he truly valued her as a person.

"What are you thinking?" Otto interrupted her musings as he returned from one of his so-called recon tours.

"Sure you want to know?"

"You had such a dreamy look on your face and I could really use some cheering up."

She giggled. "First, I need something to eat."

Otto pulled out a loaf of bread from his seemingly bottomless pocket and held it out for her, while she tore off a chunk for herself and another one for him.

"Not sure whether my thoughts are very cheerful. I just remembered the moment I finally met someone who truly loved me, and how my entire life has since gone into a downward spiral, jumping from bad to worse."

"I'm sorry." He gazed at her with his intense eyes and she felt a peculiar attraction between them. Nothing sexual, which puzzled her, because it was the only attraction she'd known from men for most of her life.

"It's not your fault. I never should have trusted Heinz in the first place."

"You and me both." Otto settled to sit beside her in the drafty freight yard where they hoped to catch a train east. Despite her initial dislike of him, a trucker and smuggler, she realized he was an honorable man. Maybe not in the traditional sense of the word but she admired his guts and the way he stuck to his principles.

"I've never thanked you for keeping me safe all this time." Bruni felt ashamed, because she'd not treated him the way he deserved.

"No need."

Otto was a puzzle to her. A rascal, but kind and caring. A man well-versed in living rough, but always on his best behavior with her. She wondered what his background was. Even after sharing so many things with him, she still had no idea who he really was, deep inside.

But she wouldn't ask him, either. Sloppy sentimentality wasn't something she readily engaged in, as she'd found it best to keep other people at arm's length.

"There should be a freight train going in our direction around midnight," he said.

Bruni had acquired some proficiency in train hopping, but she still tensed up with nerves each time. The boarding was the most dangerous part, since that was when they had to leave their cover and cross the tracks to find an unsealed wagon.

The first two or three times in the cattle cars she'd believed she saw the ghosts of the tortured souls who'd been deported to the horrible extermination camps in the east. Like most everyone else she'd closed her eyes to the atrocities committed, had chosen not to connect the dots when seeing the signs popping up – a brigade of emaciated prisoners clearing rubble after a bomb raid, Jews beaten to death on the open street, rumors of slave labor in the ammunition factories.

It was only after the downfall that the truth was dragged into the light and, in hindsight, all the pieces of the puzzle fell into place and it all made horrible sense.

"Hello Bruni and all the ships at sea, are you still here?" Otto teased her.

"I wish I weren't."

"We'll get through this, I promise. And then you can live happily ever after with your man."

"How can you promise such a thing?" Despair laced her voice and even to her own ears she sounded needy.

"We're already halfway to Hof and the Soviets are none the wiser, isn't that a good sign?"

She knew he was trying to cheer her up, but didn't have the heart to let her hopes rise. Memories of her childhood kept surfacing, destroying her will to continue this trip. It wasn't only the hunger, the cold, and the abject poverty; a hundred times more tormenting were the memories of the things her father had done to her. She thought to have left the horrors behind when she ran away and found herself one protector after another, each of them wanting the same payment in return.

"Why have you never tried to hit on me?"

Otto looked perplexed, even worried, before his face went back to normal again.

"Yes, why? What do you want in exchange for protecting me?"

"Nothing. We are in this together, aren't we?"

"Nobody does anything for free, so why are you letting me tag along? You'd be so much quicker without me." No man, except Victor, had ever stayed with her without having selfish motives. Why should Otto be any different? If he didn't want sex, then there must be something else he expected for payment.

"Bruni." Otto's voice pulled her from her reverie. "I consider you a friend. And friends help each other."

"Doesn't that sound ridiculous, even to yourself? You and me friends? That's about as likely as the sun shining at midnight."

"And yet it happened. We both aren't what we pretend to be."

"We aren't?"

"Not deep down inside." Otto was incredibly perceptive for a roughneck trucker, which maybe came with the territory of having to hide from the authorities.

"So, what is your big secret?" She pushed out her bottom lip, daring him to tell her.

"You still don't know?"

Bruni shook her head.

"I'm not into women."

Her eyes grew big and round, but words eluded her. Just like with the Nazis, the signs of Otto's preferences had been in plain sight but she had failed to connect the dots. "Oh."

CHAPTER 31

Otto had never intended to tell her his big secret, but once it was out in the open, and he'd braced himself for her derision, all she said was, "Oh."

After a long silence, she finally added, "Well, that certainly explains a few things. How could I have been so blind?"

"You're not shocked?" he asked in disbelief.

"At what? My stupidity? Or your flawless acting?"

A distant noise saved him from answering. "That should be our train. Get ready." So far, they had avoided unpleasant encounters with guards, but it was always best not to be seen loitering. Therefore, they always stayed out of sight until the train arrived, and today was no different.

The shrill brakes slowed the train to a crawl before it finally came to a stop. They'd have a few minutes to find a suitable car, while wagons were uncoupled and others coupled. It didn't take him long to spot one that wasn't properly locked. "Got one. Follow me."

This was the most dangerous part, because they had to run in plain sight across the tracks to the chosen car. Looking left and right, he waited until the freight worker disappeared behind a wagon. "Now," he hissed and sprinted away. Seconds later, he reached the railcar, jumped up and lost precious seconds opening the jammed door, before he slipped inside.

Bruni was right behind him, grabbing hold of the metal handles. He grasped the back of her overalls and swung her into the car, before they could be discovered by a pair of freight workers coming around to their side.

He fought with himself over whether he should close the door or leave it ajar, but since every movement might give them away, he whispered, "Hide in the corner until we are moving."

It took a while until his eyes adapted to the darkness and, by then, the locomotive whistled and moved out of the yard. The wagon seemed empty except for a layer of straw on the floor. He wrinkled his nose at the emerging stench. It had obviously been used to transport animals, and he hoped there wasn't a cow or pig, mad with fear, still inside. But everything was quiet, so he told Bruni to get some rest until they reached their destination in the morning.

This would be the last train hop of their journey, because the next leg had to be by foot across the green border.

"Do you think I'll ever see him again?" Bruni asked, after riding in silence for quite a while.

"You're talking about Victor, right? Of course you will. He isn't going anywhere and we should cross into the American zone within a week."

"But what then? What will we do once we are in the American zone?"

"What do you mean? You go to Wiesbaden to see Victor, and I…" He had no idea what he would do.

"That's exactly what I'm asking. We don't have valid permits for the American zone. They might arrest us, or even return us to the Soviets. I'd rather not live as a fugitive for the rest of my life."

"We'll find a way."

"But how?"

"I don't know. Can we get there first before we rack our brains about more problems?" Otto was tired, hungry, and dirty. The last time he'd taken a proper bath had been at Felix's house two weeks ago.

"I like to be prepared," Bruni said. "During this trip I've come to the conclusion that I dislike uncertainty very much."

He chuckled. No other woman in the world had the black humor she often showed. "Okay. So what do you suggest?"

"Turn ourselves in and appeal to the Americans' sense of justice? As well as to their inherent dislike for the communists. You know, my enemy's enemy is my friend."

"They will only help us if we can offer them something in return." He could not discern her face in the darkness, but certainly heard the wheels turning in her head.

"Unfortunately, that is probably true. But what do we have to offer them?" Bruni wondered. "We both look like vagabonds and have no money."

"Information."

"What kind of information?"

"I don't know." He scratched his ear. "That the so-called maintenance of the Autobahn is fake?"

"They should know that already. With their planes crossing over day and night they must have noticed the absence of construction vehicles and such."

"Yes, right. We need to keep thinking about this." His head hurt. It seemed the American zone might not be the safe haven they'd expected it to be.

The actual border crossing, two days later, was rather anti-climactic: they simply crossed somewhere in the mountainous forest area, with no patrol anywhere in sight.

Otto exhaled deeply and felt as if a heavy burden was sliding from his shoulders. He'd fulfilled his promise and delivered Bruni into the American zone. Not in Fulda as initially planned, but a good two hundred miles to the east, in Hof, close to the Czechoslovakian border.

The trip had cost him everything: his truck, his home, his mother, and his friends. One thing was clear: Otto would never be able to return into the Soviet occupied zone, if he valued his life.

"Are you sure we are in the American sector?" Bruni asked.

"Pretty sure. But we'll only know for certain once we reach the next village." He felt for the worn map in his pocket that Felix had given him just before they left for the freight depot. Despite his relief, he knew there was no reason to celebrate, since they could still be captured and returned to the Soviets. It was improbable, but a risk not to be underestimated.

Perhaps it would be better to continue his travels until he reached Genova in Italy, where he could easily find work on a ship heading to someplace far away. None of the hiring bosses would ask too many questions as long as he was willing to work hard.

"When we arrive at the village we'll find ourselves a place to sleep and wash," Bruni said with a wistful sigh.

"In that garb? They'll send us packing!" He looked at her miserable appearance. Her formerly shiny, platinum blonde hair was a dingy grayish mess and the overalls had definitely seen better times. Her face was streaked with dirt, as was the rest of her. Her ill-fitting clothing and overlarge sweater made her look like a homeless waif who'd spent her days living under a bridge.

"Not if I show them this." She pointed at her last remaining earring, the other one used to bribe a guard after they'd run out of money.

"Let's hope it's enough. The people in the West are much better off than those in Berlin or the Soviet zone."

"Gosh, how I hate those damned Soviets! Haven't we

suffered enough? But no, after so many years of war, they come along and make everything worse."

It was the first time he'd seen her throw a fit of rage and he involuntarily took a step back. "Hey, calm down." Much to his chagrin, his words had the opposite effect and she got all worked up until finally bursting into tears. Unsure what to do, he simply stood by, his arms hanging at his sides, hoping that the bundle of tears would soon get a grip on herself. He'd thought he disliked her cool aloofness but this bout of emotion was so much worse, making him wish for the cynical ice queen's return.

Fortunately for him, her outbreak didn't last long. After she'd hurled every imaginable curse word at the Russians and cried her soul out, she wiped the tears from her eyes, and said, "I must sound like a veritable battle-axe."

Otto resisted agreeing because, although he didn't know a lot about them, he'd learned this much about women: they didn't like anyone's agreement about their perceived or actual flaws. Instead he asked, "How should we go about finding a place to sleep?"

All business again, Bruni said, "We knock on the first house we come across and ask."

It might not be a good plan but at least it was a plan. They walked about an hour until they reached a street and followed it, arriving at the outskirts of a village in a matter of minutes. It was just before dusk when they knocked on the door of a lone house.

An elderly woman opened up, but before either Bruni or Otto could utter a word, she slammed the door in their faces. Seconds later, they heard the chain being secured, and muffled voices.

"That didn't work out too well," Bruni huffed. "She wouldn't even hear us out."

He had to bite back a laugh. Had she actually assumed every

villager would receive them with open arms? They could consider themselves lucky if nobody set their dogs on them. "That's because we look like tramps. She was probably afraid of us."

"You pick the next house – maybe you'll have more luck."

CHAPTER 32

They passed a few more houses, but Otto didn't stop at any one of them. Just as Bruni was getting impatient with his dawdling, they walked around a bend in the street and into the center of the village. In contrast to Berlin, here nothing had been damaged during the war. Quaint little houses lined the road leading toward the central square with a beautiful fountain in the middle.

Otto stopped at a house with the sign *"Gasthof"* – inn. It was a clever idea, because if the owner rented rooms then he was certainly used to strangers knocking at his door, albeit probably better-dressed ones.

The door opened even before they knocked, and out stepped a man in American uniform. Bruni barely managed to suppress a scream of frustration, and had to force herself to put a charming smile on her face.

"And you want?" the man asked, the weapon on his hip a stark reminder of his authority.

If they had contemplated running, the American's stance made it clear that wasn't an option. Bruni quickly assessed the situation and concluded it was best if she did the talking and not Otto, so she said, using the husky voice that had seduced many men before him, "We are looking for a place to stay a night or two."

The effect was immediately evident in the softening of his tense jawline, but not enough for him to accept them at face value. "Can I see your papers?"

"Certainly." She pulled them from the pocket of her dirty overalls, and waited until he took them before she launched into her carefully rehearsed explanation. "As you can see, I'm from Berlin."

"And your travel permit?" he asked, unimpressed.

"I'm sure you know about the awful blockade and how the Soviets are trying to kill us all?"

He gave her an impatient glance, holding out his hand for the travel permit she didn't have.

"So, yes, I escaped from Berlin without proper travel papers. I just wanted to stay alive!" She squeezed out a tear for good measure but the soldier didn't seem overly impressed, which she attributed to her awful looks. Because, who would fall at the feet of a hobo smeared with dirt from top to toe?

"What about you?" the American asked Otto, who handed him his papers, including the bill of lading to Fulda.

"Fulda? You're way off your route." The officer looked around. "Where's your truck?"

"The Soviets stole it, that's why we had to continue our journey on foot. We couldn't stay in the Soviet zone." Bruni batted her eyelashes, but to no effect.

"You're both coming to the police station with me," he said, emphasizing his words with a swift hand movement toward his weapon.

"No need for force," Bruni said. "We'll come with you. You can't imagine how glad we are to have reached the American zone because, in contrast to the Russian thugs, you are good-hearted people who value law and order."

Otto shot her a scathing gaze, which she returned and mouthed, "Let me take care of this."

The police station turned out to be on the other side of the central square, less than a five-minute walk away, which didn't give Bruni much time to consider the best forward strategy. Once inside, she asked, "Would you please allow me to use the bathroom?"

The American eyed her for a moment, before he nodded toward the end of the hallway. "Suit yourself. I'll start interrogating your partner, meanwhile. If you plan to escape, it won't end well for you both."

"Sir, I'd never even think about escaping, since I'm so happy to have gotten away from the Russian barbarians." She faked a shudder and left the two men to put her plan into action. In the small bathroom she took off the dirty sweater, washed her face and hands, and hand-combed her hair into something akin to a hairstyle. Last of all, she dug in her pockets for the most vital ingredient: the ruby-red lipstick she'd kept like a treasure throughout the journey through hell.

After carefully painting her lips, she smeared a bit of it over her cheekbones. The result wasn't perfect but it would suffice. She air kissed the mirror, cocked her head and opened the upper three buttons of her overalls, just enough to let a spectator get a glimpse of her bosom, but not enough to look cheap. Then she walked out into the reception area again, where a young soldier stared at her, his jaw sliding open.

"Hello, dear." She waved at him in the same way she did on stage. "Would you be so kind as to show me the way to your boss, please?"

"My boss?"

"Yes. He's having a conversation with a friend of mine."

"Oh...yes...of course..." He was visibly star-struck, which

gave Bruni confidence in her scheme to charm herself out of the situation.

"That is incredibly kind. You can't imagine how happy we are to have made it into the American zone...The Russians are..." She swallowed hard. "But let's not talk of these awful things. I'm safe and that is what counts, right?"

"Yes, miss." The poor lad was no match for her.

"Let me thank you for all the wonderful things you do." She stopped and put a wonderfully clean hand on his arm.

"Me?"

"Fighting the Soviets every single day, and providing food, coal or medicine to the people in Berlin."

"Oh...but I'm not...I mean... I'm not personally engaged in the airlift."

"That doesn't make it any less of a tremendous operation for humanity." She winked at him. "Although I'm sure you're being too modest."

"Here we are." The lad's face was burning bright with her flattery as he opened the door to a small office, where the officer from the Gasthof and Otto were sitting. Both men turned their heads toward the door and she could see the surprise at her transformation clearly showing on both their faces.

"Thank you so much." She peered at the name plate on his desk. "Lieutenant Dickinson. It was such a relief to be able to wash after our horrible ordeal."

"I imagine it was." Dickinson was still tight-lipped, but Bruni intended to change that.

"I'm sure this gentleman," she pointed at Otto, "who graciously agreed to help me leave Berlin in his truck, has already told you he's a smuggler?"

Dickinson's jaw tensed and Otto glared daggers at her. Of course the stupid bloke hadn't told the American. She suppressed a sigh and decided to take matters into her own hands.

"May I have a seat, please?"

"Yes." Dickinson motioned toward the chair next to Otto's.

"Can I speak frankly?" she asked and, as she had intended, the American nodded with a confused expression. It wasn't often that alleged criminals were eager to confess their sins. Bruni, though, had often had the experience that admitting a small mistake would give her a lot of leeway later on with bigger sins, and gambled on that effect.

"This man, Otto Krause, constantly travels back and forth between the Soviet zone and West Berlin to provide the population there with food, coal, medicine, and whatever else is urgently needed. If it weren't for the courageous blockade runners like him, helping the heroic airlift pilots in their near-impossible task, who knows where we would be by now? The Soviets might have gotten what they wanted and sent the other Victorious Powers running." She smiled at Dickinson. "Wouldn't that be horrendous? Not only for us suffering Berliners, but also for the rest of the free world? A precedent nobody can afford, as it might embolden the Soviets to stretch out their greedy hands and annex the western zones of Germany next."

"Now, that's maybe a bit far-fetched," Dickinson said, while Otto's eyes became wider with every word she uttered.

"And you're right to say so. I'm just a singer and entertainer who knows nothing about politics, but as it happens, I'm well acquainted with Dean Harris, the American Kommandant in Berlin, who has issued warnings for years about the Soviet hunger for territory."

Lieutenant Dickinson didn't comment on her name-dropping, but at least he'd stopped frowning. Ignoring Otto's scowl she told the American her version of what had transpired since their departure from Berlin, embellishing a few things, and leaving out some others.

In the end, he apologized profusely that they would have to

stay overnight while he discussed the matter with his superior in the next bigger town. He proceeded to offer them a shower, fresh clothes, and a proper meal, which was more than Bruni had expected.

CHAPTER 33

"Whatever did you do that for?" Otto hissed at Bruni as they were led into two adjacent cells.

"You should be grateful. Sometimes acquiescence is the best defense."

He rolled his eyes and was back to loathing her haughty arrogance. He, for one, had preferred the run-down hobo version of Bruni, but apparently that was a thing of the past. Minutes later, the young soldier returned to bring them each a blanket and clean clothes.

"Miss, I'll show you to the shower room. There's a towel and soap waiting for you, although I'm afraid we don't have shampoo."

"It will be such a joy to wash the Soviet grime off my skin, I won't even miss the shampoo." She bestowed a flashing smile on the lad, whose ears flamed into a bright red, and then she sauntered off as if this were a luxury hotel and not a goddamn prison.

Otto flopped onto his cot. Her eagerness to spill the beans would probably result in him spending years in prison, if not worse. About half an hour later, a flirtatious Bruni returned with the young soldier, who was absolutely smitten with her and only reluctantly left her behind in her cell to accompany Otto to the shower room.

He scrubbed off the grime, changed into the provided clean clothes and called for the lad to return him to his cell. Upon arrival, he noticed with surprise that a tray of food was on his cot, and Bruni was gone from her cell. Growling, he ate his meal and decided to get in a good night's sleep. In the morning, he'd discover whatever fate had in store for him.

He woke to the sound of clanking keys in the cell door.

"Get up, the C.O. wants to see you," the young soldier from the previous night said.

When he arrived at the office, there were Lieutenant Dickinson, another man with the rank of colonel...and Bruni waiting for him. She had somehow managed to scrounge a bright red dress that showcased all her female curves. She shot him a triumphant smile, and his hands itched to strangle her. He'd actually believed her to be loyal but apparently she'd chosen to hang him out to dry at the first opportunity.

"I'm Colonel Scott from the anti-smuggling division of the American Military Government." Otto's heart jumped with fear. Had this infuriating woman told them about the stolen art? Apparently she had, because Scott continued with, "We know about your cargo."

"I believed I was transporting wooden furniture," Otto said, in a defeated voice.

"Fräulein von Sinnen told us everything."

Damn woman!

"We are prepared to offer you a deal."

Otto's ears perked up. "A deal?" Maybe all was not lost and he could weasel his way out of this mess.

"Smuggling stolen artwork and cultural materials out of Berlin is not in anyone's best interests, and we've been on the tail of a particularly bold smuggling ring for years. If you are willing to expose the instigators, we are prepared to let you go free. With a residence permit in the American zone and your record of prior convictions wiped."

Otto gasped. Colonel Scott had clearly done his homework and found out about Otto's several jail sentences. Offering him a permit to stay, and a clean slate, was better than anything he could have hoped for, but there was one risk. Heinz was a man without scruples.

"If I give you the names, these people will come after me."

"Not if we keep your identity a secret," Scott offered. "We can issue a new identity for you when this is all over, if that is what you'd prefer."

Otto's gaze wandered from Scott to Dickinson and finally to Bruni, who leaned back in her chair with the expression of a satisfied cat who'd just caught a mouse.

"It's a good deal, you should take it," she said. No doubt she had orchestrated this generous offer. He preferred not to know how exactly she'd pulled it off, but was once again regretting his misjudgment of her and determined to say a big thank you as soon as they were alone.

He nodded. "Fine. Yes, I'll tell you everything I know."

"Very good. Both of you will come with me to Nuremberg for the time being, since we can't risk anyone getting wind of the issue," the colonel said.

"Colonel Scott, how can we ever thank you enough for what you have done, not only for Herr Krause and myself, but for all of Germany?" Bruni gushed.

"I'm just doing my job. We'll leave for Nuremberg in ten minutes."

Otto waited until he and Bruni had a moment alone, before he gave her a heartfelt "Thank you."

She brushed it off. "No need. I must thank you for taking such good care of me, keeping me alive against all odds, and getting me across the border."

"It was the least I could do," he mumbled.

She shook her head. "I know many men who'd have abandoned me to save their own skin. You're truly an honorable person. I hope you'll make the best of your second chance and stay away from shady business and awful people like Heinz Schuster."

Staying away from Heinz wouldn't be difficult, because when all of this was over, that man would rot in prison for quite some time. The other part, making an honest living, was much harder, but he was determined to follow in the footsteps of Felix, who'd managed to leave his criminal past behind. "I promise I won't make the same mistake a second time. I hope you and this Victor chap will lead a happy life. He is truly blessed."

"You'll find someone too. Times are changing." She kissed his cheek. "Never give up hope. Look at me, I never believed in love, and yet, here I am, crossing the bloody Soviet zone to find my man."

CHAPTER 34

Victor grabbed his crutches to walk down the hallway to the pay phone. He waited while the operator connected the call – the phone lines, for once, choosing to work when he needed them to.

"Café de Paris," a brusque voice answered.

"Yes. I need to speak with Fräulein von Sinnen," Victor said.

"We would all like to speak to her."

"What do you mean?"

"She disappeared. If you ever happen to find her, please tell her never to show up again, since she's not welcome here."

"Wait…" he pleaded into the receiver, but the person on the other end had already cut the line. He pressed the button and the operator came back on. "Get me the Café de Paris again, please."

"One moment." Static and silence greeted his request until a few moments passed and the operator's voice said, "I'm sorry, sir. There doesn't appear to be service on the lines right now. Please try your call again later."

Victor hung up the phone, feeling hopeless. Bruni hadn't shown up in Wiesbaden, and neither had she returned to Berlin.

It was a mystery. Fresh out of his wheelchair and now on crutches, he ignored the calls of his fellow patients for a game of craps and hobbled back to his room.

"There you are!" Glenn was waiting for him.

"Hello."

"I came to celebrate, since the doctors said you could leave the hospital." Glenn held up a bottle of whiskey.

"Much good it does me." Victor flopped onto the bed, exhausted after walking the short distance.

"What crawled up your ass and died there?"

"Nothing."

"So, you're just moping around for the fun of it?"

"Asshole."

Glenn smirked. "Looks like I'll have to drink my whiskey alone."

"Don't you dare! Thanks for coming, by the way." Victor struggled to sit upright. "Maybe the booze will help."

"Care to tell me the reason for your bad mood?" Glenn asked, after each of them had taken a swig from the bottle.

"Bruni."

Glenn shrugged.

"I called the Café de Paris. They have no idea where she is, she simply disappeared one day. Has Zara heard anything?"

"No, man." Glenn handed the bottle to Victor. "I'm sure there's an explanation…"

"And what might that be? If she had any intention of coming here, she'd have arrived by now. Four weeks? You could walk it in that time." Whether that was actually true or not, he didn't care.

"Maybe she got into a road accident?"

"Even in the Soviet zone they would have called her relatives." Victor took another big gulp of the strong liquid and relished the way it burned down his throat.

"Didn't you say she's estranged from her parents?"

"They could have called her friends, or her employer, or the French authorities in Berlin." Victor suddenly remembered the letter he'd given Glenn. "Has your little friend delivered the letter?"

"She went there twice but nobody opened up, so she pushed the envelope beneath the door. I'd say Bruni definitely got the letter."

"So why hasn't she responded?"

"I wish I knew."

"Because she doesn't love me, that's why!" Victor burst out, and drank some more whiskey. As far as he was concerned he'd empty the bottle and forget the world, and a certain platinum blonde woman, even existed.

Glenn seemed torn between wanting to commiserate with his friend and wanting to shake him out of his depressed mood. After a long sigh, he said, "If you want my advice: forget about her. She disappeared a month ago and hasn't given any sign of life even to her closest friends...and there's that newspaper article on how she eloped with a truck driver."

"Maybe she's in hiding?"

"Bruni? Why ever would she do that?"

"Because someone is after her?" Victor felt a sliver of hope.

"A former lover?" Glenn laughed heartily. "Sorry to be so blunt, but she's simply found another man and he promised her something you can't. It's not like she's known for being the sentimental, lovey-dovey type. Zara says relationships are nothing but a pleasant business for Bruni, meant to help her advance in life. In any case, you're cleared to leave the hospital and return stateside in a matter of days."

"I know." Victor sucked on the bottle until Glenn took it away from him.

"Can't have you dying from alcohol overdose on my watch. Forget her. It's probably for the best."

Victor didn't acknowledge Glenn's advice, nor did he

acknowledge his departure a few moments later. *It probably is for the best. Bruni wants the best and there's no way she'd want to be tied down to a man with a stiff knee. Who knows what awaits me back home? She's better off without me.*

In the afternoon, the doctor came in to give him his release papers. "Don't forget to do your physical exercises. With time and training you will be able to walk again, albeit with a cane."

"That's something to look forward to," Victor said in a sarcastic tone.

The doctor narrowed his eyes. "You should be grateful, Lieutenant. I have seen men much worse off. Your injury is a piece of cake compared to losing a limb or half your face."

"I know, Doctor. Thank you for patching me up."

"Good luck." The doctor left Victor to his own devices. But instead of hobbling over to the small locker to stuff his belongings into his kitbag, he fell on the bed and stared at the ceiling, until he heard the door again. *Can't these people leave me in peace?*

A buxom, blonde, German nurse entered with a bright smile. Victor knew she'd recently married her sweetheart, an American soldier stationed in Wiesbaden and that was exactly how she looked: elated.

"I thought you would be ready by now, Lieutenant Richards," she said in her overly chirpy voice.

"I'm not."

She might be young, but she seemed experienced enough with gloomy patients to ignore his foul mood. "Well then, I'm going to pack your belongings. There's a jeep waiting downstairs for you."

"Suit yourself." He watched her efficiently pack the few things he owned. His whole life; reduced into one kitbag. Minutes later, she finished and pushed a wheelchair in front of him. She gestured for him to have a seat. "Your chariot awaits."

"I can walk…"

"Or I can push you."

It wasn't her fault he was in this mood; she had gone out of her way to help Victor in whatever way she could. They took the elevator downstairs and, as she'd promised, there was a jeep waiting for him. "There's your ride."

She helped him into the vehicle and handed him his crutches. "Safe travels home."

"Thank you. For everything."

"You're welcome." Her bright smile was the last thing he saw before she turned the wheelchair around and headed back inside.

At the headquarters, he insisted on walking to his superior's office all by himself, even though it seemed to take an eternity and he was bathed in sweat when he finally arrived.

"Come in," his commanding officer responded after the knock.

"Sir, I was told you wanted to speak with me."

"Yes. Richards, I'll get straight to the point." The colonel picked up a sheaf of papers and waved them in the air. "These are your medical discharge documents. Are you still anxious to return stateside?"

"Yes, sir. I am." Without Bruni there was nothing keeping him in Germany.

"Well, I have good news for you. There's a C54 scheduled to return to the States for a complete overhaul. You can have a seat on that bird if you'd like."

"That would be much appreciated, sir." Victor said it without much enthusiasm. He'd been planning a life that included Bruni – without her everything seemed dull and pointless, although he would never voice that thought in the presence of his superior.

The colonel nodded at Victor's kitbag. "Is that your entire luggage?"

"Yes, sir."

"Well then. Go to the guest barracks and tell them you need

a bunk for the night. Your departure is tomorrow at sixteen hundred hours sharp."

"Yes sir, and thank you."

"We haven't been able to find the hit-and-run driver, but all signs point to the Soviets, so getting you out of Germany is best for everyone."

"I'm sure it is." Victor stood at attention and offered the colonel a salute, which was promptly returned. Then he left his boss's office and slowly hobbled across the premises to the guest quarters, where he flopped on the bed and immediately fell asleep from exhaustion. In his dreams, he found Bruni, but every time he tried to grab her hand she faded further away from him.

When he woke in the morning, he thought about seeking out Glenn to say goodbye, but resisted the urge. It was best to break with everyone and everything reminding him of his time in Germany – and of Bruni. If he wanted to have a chance to lead a happy life with another woman, he had to burn all bridges behind him. So he simply wrote a note:

Glenn,

As you may have heard already, I have returned stateside, eager to start a new life. Thanks for your help and friendship. I wish you the best of luck with Zara.

Victor.

Four years he'd been in Germany. It had seemed like such a long time, but now it was all behind him. He was headed home, determined to forget *her.*

CHAPTER 35

Finally! Bruni arrived in Wiesbaden – on a passenger train. It seemed like a lifetime ago that she'd climbed into Otto's truck in Berlin. She asked her way to the house of the Gardner family, where Zara lived and worked as their maid. Zara was in the garden with two children, playing ball, and didn't see her at first.

"Zara," Bruni called out.

"Bruni!" Zara exclaimed. "Oh, my word! You're alive and you're here!" She rushed over to open the garden gate for her friend and hugged her ferociously.

"I am here."

"You'll have to play for a few minutes without me, okay?" Zara called toward the children before she pulled Bruni inside and asked, "Where have you been? We saw the news report that you eloped with a truck driver. Victor called the Café de Paris and they said you had disappeared without a word. They are rather furious with you and told him you're not welcome to return."

Bruni had expected as much. Herr Schuster wasn't one to mess around with and he wouldn't allow such behavior even from his star singer. But she didn't care, she'd be leaving Germany soon, anyway, to live with Victor in America. Thinking of him, a warmth rushed through her veins.

"All of it is true, although maybe not in the way you think it happened. Talking of Victor, have you seen him?"

"Um...not me, just Glenn. He was in hospital until the day before yesterday, and there were no civilian visitors allowed."

"So he was discharged? Where is he now? I'll go straight to see him."

Zara's face grew solemn. "He flew out."

"Flew out? Where to?" Bruni's vision blurred. Victor was afraid of flying, so why on earth would he voluntarily fly anywhere?

"You must understand. He was heartbroken when he saw the news report and heard the rumors about you eloping with the truck driver..."

"Eloping? I didn't elope with him. He was supposed to get me across the border," Bruni cried out, as her brain tried to process the news. It couldn't be true. No, he wouldn't. Never. Not Victor. "Tell me you didn't believe such nonsense. I mean, imagine...me with a trucker? Why would anyone who knows me believe such nonsense?"

"You'd been gone for so many weeks and no one had heard from you...People fill in the blanks," Zara stated.

"What a miserable slimebag!" Bruni yelled, and stomped her foot – clad in a shiny high heel. "I've just thrown away a month of my life to see him and what does the low-life rat do? He packs up and returns to the land of opportunity! Leaving me on a whim, just because some stupid tabloid told some outrageous lies! Who does he think he is?"

Zara stood in silence until Bruni stopped ranting. "Want some coffee?"

"Hell, yes! I hope you have real coffee because I don't think I need any more bad news today." She opened her purse to take out a cigarette, fondly thinking of Colonel Scott who had provided her with the new clothes, shoes, accessories, and makeup in exchange for her contribution to finding the stolen art pieces.

"You need to calm down, Mrs. Gardner does not approve of swearing in her house." Zara busied herself making coffee, while Bruni lit her cigarette. Victor's betrayal had cut deeply into her soul, but before she could wallow in self-pity, Zara asked, "What really happened once you left Berlin?"

Bruni opened her mouth to tell her friend the truth, but she'd promised Colonel Scott absolute discretion, or he would have kept her in Nuremberg until they captured the smugglers. So she made up a fantastic story about Otto promising to take her to Wiesbaden and how his truck had broken down and they'd had to stay with his mother. She made it sound exciting and incredible, and she could tell that Zara wasn't buying a word of it.

"Just stop telling me your fantasy story. It doesn't matter, I for one am incredibly happy to see you're safe."

"Me too."

Zara served two cups of coffee and a plate of brownies at the kitchen table. Just as she sat down, Bruni became aware of the ring on her friend's finger. She reached for Zara's hand and asked, "Is this what I think it is?"

Zara blushed and held up her hand, allowing the ring to be fully displayed. "Glenn asked me to marry him, and I said yes."

"Congratulations." Bruni pulled her in for another hug. "You have chosen well. Let's hope your guy doesn't pack up and escape to America at the first doubt about your relationship."

"I'm so sorry."

"No need to be sorry for me, I'm just glad I found out about his true colors before we got married." It was a lie, but Bruni would rather be dead than admit she was crushed to the core.

After drinking her coffee, she said, "I'd better go, your employers won't appreciate me keeping you from work."

"What will you do?"

"I'll stay in a hotel for a few nights and consider my options. Until the blockade is lifted I won't be able to return to Berlin, and we don't know how long it will go on for."

"Oh. I hadn't thought about that." Zara accompanied Bruni outside, where the children were playing in the garden. "Would you like Mrs. Gardner to ask around for a job for you? She is very well-connected."

"Your employer, or her female friends, probably have different ideas about suitable jobs for me than I do." Bruni giggled.

"I guess that's right. Meet me tomorrow after dinner, we can go out for a drink and I'll introduce you to some people who might help. There's quite a vibrant nightlife in Wiesbaden."

"Now that sounds like a plan." Bruni waved goodbye.

She decided to try her luck at the barracks where maybe she could find out some more about Victor. But the only information she was given was that yes, Lieutenant Richards had left for the States and no, they didn't know which city, and no, they didn't have an address either.

It was almost as if he'd never existed. Her entire future lay shattered like broken glass. Once she was out of the guard's sight she stomped her foot furiously and cried out, "You're dead to me, Victor Richards! Miserable traitorous swine! I hope you'll regret this for the rest of your life!"

Feeling slightly better after her outburst she walked to the city center in search of a nice, yet affordable hotel. Soon she would have a new job and a new benefactor, but right now she had to tighten her belt.

CHAPTER 36

For the past month, Otto had been at the American military headquarters in Nuremberg every single day. He'd been interrogated by at least half a dozen different intelligence agents and had repeated over and over every single detail he knew about the operation.

From what he had gleaned so far, Heinz Schuster was one of the heads of the smuggling ring, and Otto couldn't wait to get his revenge on the man who'd almost ruined his life.

One day Otto was summoned to Colonel Scott's office. After a brief greeting, the colonel cut right to the chase. "We've got them. Head of the snake, as well as the tail. All in all, about two dozen men. They led us to a warehouse in Berlin stuffed with jewelry, artwork, gold, antiques, you name it. Mostly priceless and unique pieces stolen by the Nazis all over Europe."

"That was quick work," Otto said.

"Without your inside information we couldn't have done it."

"I'm glad I could help."

"There is one more thing we need and then your part in this operation will be officially over."

"What's that?"

"I need you to positively identify the man who commissioned you to move the two shipments of furniture and artifacts."

A shiver crept down Otto's spine at the notion of having to face Heinz. People like him were like roly-poly dolls who always bounced back. He'd rather not meet him face to face.

Scott seemed to have noticed Otto's reluctance and said, "No worries. He won't see you. He'll be behind a one-way mirror, so you can see him, but not the other way round."

"Okay." A heavy stone fell from Otto's heart.

"There will be six men, and you need to give me the number of the one who hired you for that cargo of furniture. Understood?"

He nodded and followed the colonel into another room, where three American officers waited for them. One of them repeated the instructions and asked Otto whether he understood and swore to give a truthful answer.

He affirmed on both accounts. Next thing the lights went on behind the wall, which turned into a see-through window. Six men were marched in and lined up against the wall.

Otto's eyes immediately locked on Heinz. The man was standing among the others, attempting to look bored and disinterested in what was happening around him, but Otto wasn't fooled. Fear lurked in Heinz's eyes.

"That's Heinz Schuster. The second man from the left. He contracted me to transport furniture to Fulda."

All four men in the room were exceptionally pleased and the one who'd given him the instructions earlier said, "That should do it. Thanks for your help."

"You're welcome."

Colonel Scott motioned for Otto to follow him and later offered him a seat in his office. "Again, thanks for your cooperation."

"It actually wasn't my idea. You know, a man with my background has difficulties trusting the authorities."

Scott grinned. "Well, then I should probably thank your lady friend. She's a smart cookie."

"She certainly is."

"Have you given any thought to where you want to begin a new life?"

Otto had given this a lot of thought during the past month and since he didn't have any preferences of location, he'd opted to go where the work was. "Yes, sir. I was planning to try my luck in the Ruhr area. I've heard they need plenty of drivers for the coal mines and, if I know one thing, it's how to drive a truck."

"Good choice. It's the up-and-coming industrial area in Germany and you're right, labor is what they are short of. It'll take a few days for my colleagues to issue permits for the British zone because, you know, independency and all that."

Three days later, Otto was sitting in a train headed to Essen, fully equipped with forty German marks, a new set of clothes, and a permanent residency permit for the American and British bizone.

He determined that as soon as he'd gotten on his feet, he'd start sending money to his mother, and maybe one day he could bring her to live with him.

CHAPTER 37

Four years later

"And the lovely Brunhilde von Sinnen will be delighting concert goers, young and old alike, as she continues her first United States tour. Tickets are available and can be purchased at the venue. Don't wait until the last minute – her shows have been selling out across the country."

Victor stopped what he was doing and stared at the radio sitting on the counter. A moment later, the radio announcer's voice came back on.

"Miss von Sinnen has graciously agreed to sing a song for us live, right now. The airwaves are all yours, my dear."

"Thank you, Jack. This song is for every man and woman who have found the love of their lives, and for those who are still seeking."

Bruni's remarkable voice filled the air as she launched into the song she'd sung the first night Victor laid eyes on her at the Café de Paris, *I'm in the Mood for Love*.

Victor's heart filled with emotion as he sang along with her, remembering every precious minute he'd spent with the woman who still owned his heart. Because, despite his best intentions, he'd never managed to forget her or even maintain more than a superfluous relationship with another woman.

As the song came to an end, his entire being ached for her. Bruni was in the States and now that he'd heard her voice, he absolutely had to see her again.

It was a foolish idea. Knowing how she enjoyed basking in men's admiration all over the world, she had surely found one to keep her warm these past years. But he still hoped she'd give him the explanation he'd hungered for since the day he'd read that newspaper article about her eloping with a truck driver.

He called the radio station and, after being passed from person to person, was finally able to find out Bruni's tour schedule. She'd give a concert in his city ten days from now. He rushed out to buy a ticket at the venue, but the nearer the day drew, the more doubts he had.

The night of the concert, he decided to stay home. He wouldn't make a fool of himself pining for a woman who'd left him without a word. But mere moments later, he changed his mind again. He'd go and listen to her sing; she'd never have to find out that one of the men in the audience was him.

He dressed in his best suit and tie, stopped at the local floral stand and picked up a bouquet of red roses. After much consideration he wrote *From an old friend in Berlin* onto the card and handed it to the ticket-taker at the venue, who promised to see that Miss von Sinnen received it.

Victor almost lost heart when he saw the pile of flower bouquets waiting to be delivered to her dressing room. But then again, he didn't actually expect to see her. All he wanted was to hear her mesmerizing voice one more time before he closed this chapter of his life, once and for all.

During the show it was as if he was transported years back into the Café de Paris where he'd so often seen her perform. Her sultry alto voice poured over his senses like the finest alcohol, smooth and potent.

He watched as she sashayed across the stage and down the stairs, shaking hands with the audience in the first row. She drew out the last chorus of the love song, while moving along the patrons and up onto the stage again on the other side. She held the last note for what seemed like an eternity and for a split-second he met her eyes and believed he saw recognition in them, although that was impossible.

The audience gave standing ovations and he automatically sprung to his feet with everyone else, clapping his hands to demand an encore, which she graciously granted. Victor, though, forgot everything around him and remembered when she'd sat on his lap whispering sweet words into his ear. Shivers ran down his spine and he barely noticed that most of the concertgoers had filed out of the auditorium.

Drawn by the intense desire to wrap his arms around her, he walked up onto the stage and slid behind the heavy black curtain. He followed the sound of voices and found himself in a narrow hallway with several doors leading off each side. Uncertain as to what exactly he was about to do, he paused. From the other side of the hallway someone came toward him, almost completely hidden behind flower bouquets, stopped in front of a door and knocked. After delivering the flowers, the woman retreated the way she had come.

Before his courage could leave him, Victor walked toward the door with a slight limp that always got worse when he was nervous or tired, and knocked.

* * *

BRUNI WAS SITTING in front of a large mirror, touching up her makeup, dressed in a pink satin robe. She was exhausted from two hours performing on stage, but also elated. The audience had been amazing. Standing up there with thousands of patrons cheering her on always gave her a thrill that compared to nothing else.

The only other time in her life she'd felt a similar elation had been with Victor – but he'd dumped her like a hot potato, believing the drivel written about her eloping with Otto. Even two years later her heart still ached.

She shrugged. The past was the past. Victor had shattered her heart, and she'd put it back together badly, reinforcing her conviction that men couldn't be trusted and that she was better off looking out for herself. Marlene and Zara had both tried to coax her into finding Victor, while touring America, but she had fought them tooth and nail. She wouldn't be able to endure it if she discovered he was happily married to someone else.

No, it was preferable not to know what had become of him.

A knock on the door interrupted her musings and she said, "Come in." Expecting another delivery of flowers she didn't bother to turn around, and instead finished applying eyeshadow.

When the visitor didn't say anything, and she didn't hear footsteps either, she slowly swung around on her swivel chair and froze. Her mind was playing tricks on her; it couldn't be Victor. But it was him, in the flesh, all the way to the devastating twinkle in his eyes, and even more handsome than she remembered.

It took her an eternity to recover from the shock, but she finally managed to ask, "Are you the friend from Berlin?"

His gaze went to the roses standing in a vase beside her and he nodded. She got up, coming to stand several feet away from him, both of them at a loss for words. As much as she had loathed him for dumping her all that time ago, she couldn't prevent the overwhelming rush of exhilaration rising inside her.

"Your performance tonight was amazing," he said, his deep voice washing over her, threatening to sweep her away.

"You were in the audience?" She had to hold on to her sanity, couldn't let herself fall for him again, so she wrapped her arms around her middle and took a step back.

"Yes. After hearing about your tour on the radio last week I knew I had to come and see you."

"But why? You dumped me." Fury rose in her throat, as she was forced to relive the pain, the sorrow, the fear of arriving in Wiesbaden after her ordeal and finding out he'd already left.

"Because you were...are you happy with him?" Victor wrung his hands, seemingly as disturbed as she was by their reunion.

Her eyes bulged in anger. "So you believed that drivel? You of all persons? The one man in the world I opened my heart to? You tore it out and trampled on it!"

A multitude of expressions were reflected on his face. Shock, sadness, regret, shame. For years she'd hoped he'd never be happy again, that he would realize he had committed the worst error in his life by abandoning her. But now, all those feelings of revenge were gone.

"Bruni...I...I was in a very bad place after my accident. When you disappeared I was sick with worry, and then...those news reports...please...I have to know...what really happened?" When she pressed her lips into a thin line, he fell to one knee, holding the other leg slightly to the side, and begged, "I now realize I was a fool to let you go without a fight."

"An asshole would be a more fitting description," she said coldly. She was moved by his gesture, but wouldn't forgive him this easily.

"Whatever you call me, you're probably correct."

"You can get up. What happened to your knee?"

"It's been stiff since the accident. I can't bend it more than thirty degrees."

"Would you like some champagne? To remember the good times we had?" She needed a distraction or she'd throw herself at him like some adoring puppy.

"That would be nice."

Bruni led him to a coffee table with two plush seats and poured champagne into glasses. "What should we toast to?"

"How about the most stupid man on earth who let the only woman he ever truly loved go?"

Her hand trembled slightly as she raised her glass and took a sip. "You want to know what really happened?" He nodded. "I'll tell you. I was sworn to secrecy, but I think we're far enough away and by now it's all water under the bridge anyway."

His eyes never left her face and with every passing second, she regretted the lost time more. If only she'd listened to her friends and looked for him.

"I left Berlin in search of you, because I feared if they sent you home before I found you, I'd never see you again. Which is exactly what happened," she said bitterly, gulping down her glass of champagne and refilling it. "The trip didn't proceed as planned. Otto, the trucker you were so jealous about, was duped into smuggling stolen art. The Soviets caught him and threw us both in prison."

Victor swallowed hard, his ears reddening. "My poor darl...Bruni. I'm such a bloody idiot."

"Yes, you are." His admission gave her some satisfaction but not in the way she'd hoped. "We managed to escape and what followed was an arduous journey through the Soviet zone, always hiding from authorities. It's a time I never want to relive or remember, but I finally arrived in Wiesbaden, exactly one day after you'd flown out."

"I'm so sorry." Victor looked genuinely contrite, and he should be, because he'd thrown away their chance for happiness and true love because...because of what, exactly? "I was an idiot. I should have had faith in you."

"Yes, you should," she said, pouring herself a third glass.

He took the bottle from her hand and cupped her cheek. "My wonderful, brave darling. Will you forgive me, please?"

"I don't know if I can. You broke my heart, shattered me. It took me months to get myself back together ...Nobody knew or even guessed, but my life felt pointless without you. There were days I wanted to fall asleep and never wake up again."

His voice trembled as he said, "I can only repeat how sorry I am. I was utterly stupid. And there's no excuse for that. I should have known to listen to my heart rather than what the newspapers published. I was so jealous, I couldn't think clearly...forgetting you seemed to be the best solution – return to the States and start a new life. But I never could. I've missed you every single day for the past years."

Instead of an answer, she closed her eyes and when she opened them again, a tear slid down her cheek. "Why did you never look for me?"

"Because I was afraid. I couldn't stand the idea of seeing you happy with another man."

"So why did you come today?"

"Honestly? I didn't want to. I almost pulled out of coming to the concert at least a dozen times today, but I told myself I'd just listen to your voice one more time; you'd never know I was there. But the moment I saw you on the stage, singing our song, the time slipped away and I was back in Berlin in the Café de Paris, where I saw you for the first time. I had to talk to you, find out whether you are happy."

"I'm not." Tears were streaming down her face, an entirely unusual emotion for her.

"Please, will you let me make you happy again? Give us a second chance?" He didn't wait for an answer, but pulled her into his arms. She offered merely a token protest, before she melted against him, her tears soaking his jacket.

"I love you, my darling," he said.

"I love you, too. So much. You ripped my heart apart."

"How can I make it up to you? "

Bruni slipped from his embrace. "I'm not sure I could go through this a second time."

"You won't have to. I'll never doubt you again. These past years were so miserable, I never want to wake up without you by my side ever again." Victor took a tentative step toward her, wiped her tears away with his thumbs and then lowered his head and kissed her.

"I never loved anyone but you," she mumbled against his lips.

AUTHOR'S NOTES

Dear Reader,

Thank you so much for reading Into the Unknown. If you did enjoy it, and want to keep up-to-date with all my latest releases, just sign up at the following link. Your email address will never be shared and you can unsubscribe at any time.

https://kummerow.info/

Many of you wrote me how much they loved Bruni and her devil-may-care attitude and wanted to know what became of her and Victor. I already had the perfect story for her in mind, since I wanted to put her through the things she hates most: the ugly side of life everyone else in Berlin has to cope with and that she's worked so hard to avoid.

As always, a book forms in my mind by putting together several snippets of information. One of them was a newspaper article from January 1949, where the headquarters of the US Air Force in Europe announced the uncovering of a huge smuggling ring that was said to have moved jewels, precious metals and high-value industrial products with a total value of several million US dollars from Germany to foreign countries.

Heinz Schuster was the obvious culprit, because of his exposed position in the Café de Paris. Then, I read in Frank L. Howley's memoir Berlin Command (he was the American Commandant in Berlin during the airlift and has inspired my Dean Harris), about his encounter with a German proposing smuggling. You can read my take on how that encounter might have happened in Chapter 6 where Heinz visits Dean.

And there I had my idea. Where things are smuggled into Berlin, there's also a way to smuggle things out of Berlin. Now I just needed a counterpart for Bruni. Otto was perfect, because he's everything she's not, and he challenges her in a way nobody else could.

Unfortunately I haven't found any primary sources about either the blockade runners, or art smugglers, so most of that part is fiction. What is true, though, are the increasing tensions between East and West, the clamping down on any transport between not only the Western zones and Berlin, but also between East and West Germany, and the tightening of restrictions in the Soviet zone, where Stalinism was implemented and any criticism persecuted.

My editor asked my why neither Bruni nor Victor searched for each other after the separation and the simple answer is: it was not possible. We can't compare the conditions with today, when any information is just a click away.

Even inside Germany with the Red Cross having long lists of thousands upon thousands of missing people, it could take years to find displaced family members, but there was no such search service in place in America. Moreover, the US army was very reluctant to give out information about their soldiers. This was usually done to protect them from paying alimony, because men who found themselves in such a situation were whisked away stateside and the mother was never given information about the father's whereabouts. There are countless stories of children who only learned about their real father decades later.

THANKS again for reading Into the Unknown, and I would immensely appreciate it if you found the time to leave a review.

Marion Kummerow

ALSO BY MARION KUMMEROW

Love and Resistance in WW2 Germany

Unrelenting

Unyielding

Unwavering

War Girl Series

Downed over Germany (Prequel)

War Girl Ursula (Book 1)

War Girl Lotte (Book 2)

War Girl Anna (Book 3)

Reluctant Informer (Book 4)

Trouble Brewing (Book 5)

Fatal Encounter (Book 6)

Uncommon Sacrifice (Book 7)

Bitter Tears (Book 8)

Secrets Revealed (Book 9)

Together at Last (Book 10)

Endless Ordeal (Book 11)

Not Without My Sister (Spin-off)

Berlin Fractured

From the Ashes (Book 1)

On the Brink (Book 2)

In the Skies (Book 3)

Into the Unknown (Book 4)

Margarete's Story

Turning Point (Prequel)

A Light in the Window

Historical Romance

Second Chance at First Love

Find all my books here:

http://www.kummerow.info

Made in United States
North Haven, CT
05 May 2022

18914074R00126